Fifty Years
of
Eternal Vigilance

Fifty Years
of
Eternal Vigilance

AND OTHER STORIES

Carolyn Thorman

PEACHTREE PUBLISHERS, LTD.
ATLANTA · MEMPHIS

Published by
Peachtree Publishers, Ltd.
494 Armour Circle, N.E.
Atlanta, Georgia 30324

Manufactured in the United States of America
10 9 8 7 6 5 4 3 2 1

Design by Lisa Lytton-Smith
Illustrations by Lisa Lytton-Smith and Rusty Smith

Library of Congress Catalog Card Number 88-61458

ISBN 0-934601-62-3

The stories in this collection were written in part under
literary work-in-progress grants awarded in 1984 and 1987
from the Maryland State Arts Council.

"God Giving Lithuania to the World" first appeared in *Story Quarterly;*
"Fifty Years of Eternal Vigilance" in *Southern Exposure;* "Society for the
Benefit of the Daughters of Vilnius" in *The Connecticut Writer;* "No Job
Too Small" in *The Antietam Review;* "Binkas Sausage" in *The Saint
Andrews Review;* "Anchovy Trees" in *The Pennsylvania Review;*
"Gurlas" in *The Memphis State Review;* "Sweet Chickadee of Grace" in
The Madison Review; and "Blue Haired Chickens" in *Plainswoman.*

Look at me, Helena

Picking luck

As if it grew wild

CONTENTS

ONE

God Giving Lithuania to the World

The more people I pay to buy Vito's paintings so he thinks he's a great artist, Galina Restinas thought, the more danger he'll find out. She glanced at the kitchen clock and lowered the gas under the borscht. For two years Vito had come for dinner every Friday night and left Sunday afternoon. Whenever he finished a painting, he would bring it along. After they ate, they would clink glasses of kummel, then have the unveiling.

She supposed if Vito ever said, 'Let's get married,' she'd say, "Why not?" But, she thought, adjusting the venetian blinds to a squint, trying to squirrel that man into anything was like trying to get a cat from under a bed.

It was getting dark. Maybe she should call him up and say you're this late so stay home and eat salami. Home was five Baltimore row houses

1

away, with the same stained glass lilies over the entrance and the same popeyed flamingoes painted on the screen door. The only difference was that the marble steps leading to her stoop had an ivory patina, like dentures, from her weekly scrubbings. Vito's hadn't been scoured since his wife died ten years ago. That was about the same time Louie Restinas passed from a stroke while shoveling coal at Number Nine Bessemer Furnace.

"Being retired is better for your heart," she advised Vito.

"In my true soul I was never a carpenter anyway," he told her, and everyone who came to look at his paintings.

Except for Cloris Mikalouskas and Staffey Retski, everyone left without buying. Galina had made a deal with those two to pay for any picture they picked out and let them keep it, providing they kept their mouths clamped tight as oysters. I had to do something, she told herself, to keep his courage up.

She was tearing May off the Kozsciewskow Savings and Loan calendar when the front door rattled. "Come straight in," she yelled.

Vito's voice was muffled. "Give me a hand."

She bustled through the living room to the jalousie door and set the stop on the cylinder to keep it open. He struggled over the sill with a canvas wrapped in patched A&P bags. "Must be six feet tall," she said.

"Watch the top," he said, angling it through the doorway. She steadied one end while he lowered the canvas against the living room wall.

"I should have gone to your place," she said.

He held his baseball cap by the peak and mopped his brow. "Has to be here first for luck." He kissed her cheek. "Dinner ready?"

"Has been for an hour."

"Guess I was wrapping. I smell borscht." He followed her into the kitchen.

She glanced up at him. He looks older every day, she thought. In pretty good shape except for his blue eyes that looked as if they had been thickened with cornstarch. He'd been sleeping in his clothes again—his navy shirt was shaggy with silver hairs from his mongrel, Queen Hedwig.

He peered into the pot. "Those beets look like peaches," he said, rubbing his hand down her chubby thigh.

"Boiling, waiting for you."

He stooped to slide his hand under her dress. She pretended not to notice while she leaned against his palm. He drew the dress to the top of her white stockings. (Like Lady Diana's, she had explained to him.) They were twisted in a knot on top because she believed garters caused cancer. Vito popped the knot loose.

"Now what have you done?" she giggled.

His fingers slid over her underwear. She brought her knee up to pinch his hand. "You want this soup now or don't you?"

His fingers paused, scuttled to the corner of her thigh, then snapped the leg band on her pants goodbye. "Only had salami for lunch," he sighed.

She tied up her stocking, then loaded the formica table with steaming platters. "Eat."

"Stomach's a bowling ball."

"You're just scared I won't like the painting."

"Talk about anything else, please."

His nerves are tight as new clothesline when he brings a picture, she remembered. "Peppi De Vencenzio stopped by this afternoon with a better price for my Conkling Street building. I said forget it."

Vito glanced up from the comma-shaped pork chop he was gnawing. "Sell and be done with it."

"I don't want his noisy sister, Mafalda, opening her pizza joint on our street. With hoodlums stealing hubcaps all night."

"Then keep on talking Peppi into your Fleet Street big loser. Let Mafalda steal hubs over there." Vito held up the empty vodka bottle. "Got any more?"

He must have a hole in his throat, she thought and reached into the enamel cabinet for a new fifth. She watched him wash down the last ruffle of cabbage. "Finished?" she asked, lifting his plate.

He got up, stretched, and went to the china

closet. He took out two stemmed glasses, the kummel, and bumped the door shut with his elbow. "Hurry up in the kitchen," he yelled.

She hung her bibbed apron on the broom closet door and patted her new permanent. She hoped the black smudges on her scalp from hair color didn't show.

Vito, a master of ceremonies, was waiting in the living room. He pointed to the orange vinyl chair. "Sit down here," he ordered. He reached for the lampshade on the head of the Chinese lady with the clock in her stomach, and tipped it toward the wrapped canvas. Galina folded her hands on her lap while he poured kummel. "Sveikas" they said, clinking glasses.

He wiped his mouth on his sleeve while striding to the canvas. With a swoop of his pocketknife, he cut the string, tore off the paper and kicked it aside.

She stared at the glistening umber oak trunks. One could almost hear the leaves rustle, owls whoop, frogs splash in the left corner.

"Beautiful," she sighed.

"There's Danalaikas' house with the stork nest on top," he said.

She walked over to examine the center. "Puntukas!" she exclaimed, recognizing the legendary rock. She turned to ask, "What's the picture's name?"

"God Giving Lithuania to the World."

She stared at the tiny patch of sky. "Where's God?"

He shrugged, looking helpless. "Was too big."

She nodded. A genius, she thought. But who's buying great art in Baltimore? Mrs. Spassky next door had plenty of framed embroidered kittens on velvet. Father Abrovaitas already had an oil picture of Saint Isidore's Cathedral in Vilnius.

Vito paced between the kitchen door and sofa. He stopped to admire the painting each time he passed. "Not selling to just anybody the way I did the others. This is the work of my life. Maybe for a museum, some important building where there are big crowds night and day."

"And how!" she said as she filled his glass. "Meanwhile, you might as well calm down."

Three hours later, in bed, with Vito's knee poking her hip, she listened to thunder growling over the Chesapeake a few blocks away.

Even if I did decide to help Vito, she brooded, I don't know any big shots who would hang his picture. Besides, it's no good for him to think he's getting somewhere when he's not.

Then she saw his wizened fingers, hand spotted like a brown Dalmatian as he clutched the brush. He was running out of time. Next place, his work could be propped around him in Skardas' Funeral Parlor. I might go to the poorhouse buying them—but so what? Skardas is close to getting my business too. Galina gazed at the picture of the Blessed Mother lit by the street light. One good thing about being my age, she sighed, is the cost of love doesn't matter any more.

Rain clicked against the window Monday morning as she sat at the kitchen table sorting rent receipts. Vesky's money order was late again she grumbled as the doorbell clanged. She peeked out the living room window between the statue of Saint Francis and "Vote for Kalaikas" poster to see who was on the stoop.

"Mr. De Vencenzio," she said opening the door.

"Mrs. Retsina," the fat man smiled.

"Restinas." She motioned him to the sofa as he propped his umbrella near the door.

"Some drops," he apologized.

"Think nothing of it," she said, checking the carpet.

"I talked to Mafalda after Mass. She has enough from Tony's insurance to ask you one more time . . ."

"I'll show you Fleet Street right now."

"Give you fifty-five for Conkling," he said, higher than she thought he'd go.

"I'm thinking."

He frowned at his watch. "I have a city council meeting in half an hour."

All at once her mind rolled up a plan the way her fingers rolled cabbage leaves around barley. I would have figured this out before, she thought, but when you get old, your head has to strain like a truck climbing Petrovsky Street.

7

"You want Conkling at fifty-five? Take it."

He stopped smiling. "Why a change?"

She sat in the wicker chair across from him. "For a favor. You donate my friend's oil painting and put it up in City Hall."

Peppi hunched his shoulders up the sides of his neck. "I don't want to buy no picture."

"I'm buying, you're hanging."

"Even so, you think I can hang pictures in City Hall like in my living room?"

"Okay, so fix it for some other famous building." She tipped her chair toward him. "Look at it this way. For no cost you can throw a big dedication ceremony. Invite Congresslady Kalaikas."

Peppi's eyes narrowed. "Let me get everything straight. You give me a picture, I get a dedication and Conkling at fifty-five."

"Only you have to pretend to be buying the picture from my friend, Mr. Lapidauskas."

Peppi jumped up and strode around the room waving his arms. "I make my Easter duty and what thanks do I get? Crazies who ask me to waste my time making a fool of myself." He stopped and grinned. "Hey, I bet I know why you're up to this." She felt her face flush kielbasa red. Peppi held up his hand. "How fast will you close?"

"One minute after the picture goes up."

Two weeks later, Vito and Galina sat in her kitchen. Vito propped his elbows on the formica table. "What makes you think Peppi's going to buy my painting?" he asked.

"Told you one thousand times. When Peppi made the fifty-five offer he mentioned wanting to donate something to look good before the election. I said, 'Why not an oil painting?' So he said he'd come take a look."

Vito closed his watery eyes. "Bet he wants it for City Hall. I feel fame lifting my heart like a derrick."

"Don't count your chickens," Galina said as she punched a hole in the top of a can of condensed milk with a butcher knife.

"Why not? I worked like animal all my life." He watched her pour his coffee. The doorbell rang.

Galina ushered Peppi into the kitchen. "Mr. De Vencenzio, Mr. Lapidauskas." The men shook hands.

"You live around here?" Peppi asked.

"Five doors down," Vito said. Peppi beamed and pumped Vito's hand harder.

"Coffee?"

"No, thank you very much. I'm on the run."

"Picture's in here," Galina said as the men followed her into the living room.

Vito motioned Peppi to the vinyl chair and snapped on the Chinese lamp. The shade was already tilted into place. The canvas was facing the wall. Galina helped Vito swing it around to face Peppi. Vito tensed while the councilman studied the picture. "Very nice trees," Peppi said. "What's that?"

Vito leaned to follow Peppi's finger pointing to the center.

"Puntukas Rock," Vito said. "Devil was dropping it on the village of Anykščiai before the sacred oaks stopped him. That's why the picture's called "God Giving Lithuania to the World."

"God in there?" Peppi asked.

"Wasn't room."

"A very fine work, Mr. Lapidauska. . . . How much?"

"Who can say," Vito said as he shrugged his bony shoulders. "Maybe thousand dollars?"

Peppi whistled and glanced at Galina, who frowned and jerked her head in a quick 'no' behind Vito's back. Just yesterday, she recalled, Vito said great artists are supposed to die poor.

"Two fifty?" Peppi asked.

"You're insulting me. Not less than three."

Galina caught Peppi's eye and nodded.

"Three's a deal!" Peppi held out his hand and they shook again.

Vito beamed and rubbed his palms together. "Mrs. Restinas said you wanted this picture for City Hall."

Peppi made a sweeping motion. "Much better. This is to be a gift to the people of our neighborhood. Have already made arrangements . . ." Galina shot him a warning look. "Promised Captain Verdi I'd contribute a work of art to his building."

"The Southeast Police Station?" asked Vito.

"Is wonderful," Galina said at Vito's scowl. "Just think, people coming and going night and day."

"True," Vito said.

"We'll throw a big dedication ceremony," Peppi added.

"Mayor be there?" Vito asked.

"I'll invite him," Peppi said as he turned toward the door. "Call you with details. It has been a real pleasure."

Galina shut the door behind him. Vito leaped beside Galina and kissed her cheek. "And you said not to count chickens," he said and laughed.

"You're a lucky man."

He held up his hands and wiggled his fingers. "Not luck, skill. You spot De Vencenzio's face when he saw it?"

She watched Vito strut in front of the painting.

"Got anything to eat?" he asked.

As she opened the refrigerator she felt let down. Might have been a wrong move to cheat him out of the struggle to sell his work on his own. Her three hundred dollars maybe just stuffed his head, not his confidence. But what did I expect, she thought. If I had wanted thanks, I should never have invented this deal. "How about a little celebration?" she yelled to Vito. "Got a roaster from Santoni's."

11

He came in from the living room while she tied on her apron. He swung a chair from under the table and sat on it backwards. "Who should come to the dedication?"

"Father Abrovaitas," she said.

"He won't unless the mayor comes."

She paused and sliced into an onion. "He will if Kalaikas asks him."

The dedication wasn't until one o'clock. Plenty of time, Galina thought. She sliced souri cheese and arranged Ritz crackers on a styrofoam tray labeled, "Stans . . . Bar of Distinction." Better take enough for fifty, she figured. She took a last look at the packed supplies—food, iced tea, and vodka, in case someone asked. Then she went upstairs to slip on her black taffeta dress and gold wedgies. Downstairs, she tied a bouffant net over her varnished curls. Better take a taxi with this load, she decided, lifting one carton and realizing it would take at least three trips to get it down the front steps.

She tipped the cab driver to load the cartons and pile them inside the door of the police station. There was Vito slumped on a bench at the end of the hall. "No one will come," he said. He was wearing his only suit, red and green checks, and his usual navy shirt.

She hurried to the folding table the captain set up and began to put out paper plates and cups. "Only fifteen minutes to one," she said.

"Why bother for nothing?" he asked, adjusting his white tie.

The bar on the door clanked open and Father Abrovaitas swept in, hair gleaming like a new dime, cassock whirling as he rounded the corner. "Anyone here?" he asked.

"Kalaikas has a speech at the Slavic Knights of Columbus in Dundalk," Galina said. "Mayor's on board the Port Welcome."

The priest's shoulders dropped. He nodded to the wrapped canvas beside Vito. "Where's it going to be hung?"

"Not sure yet," Vito replied.

The door clanked again and Mafalda and her kids tumbled into the corridor like marbles from a broken bag. "Don't give me no shit!" Mafalda yelled, whacking at one scrambling up the water fountain. Father Abrovaitas winced.

Peppi, looking at his watch, bounded in, as Jay-Jay Jandoli, the probate judge, approached their group. Mrs. Spassky entered with her bug-eyed chihuahua, Acapulco, shivering against her sweater. Next, three ladies came from the Society for the Benefit of the Daughters of Vilnius, and finally, Charlie Skardas, dressed to the teeth.

From the other end of the corridor, a green rippled glass door opened, and Captain Verdi sauntered down the hall, pulling his belt over his stomach as he neared the crowd. "Let's get this show on the road," he barked. Peppi grabbed his arm and the captain bent to hear him whisper, then stood erect. "Everybody follow me," he ordered. The crowd straggled behind him into a waiting area marked, "Traffic Adjudication."

Galina looked around the gloomy green room with rows of benches facing a window with a round hole. An old woman with yellowed gray hair frizzed under a tattered beret dozed against a bench. Across from her was a man wearing a canvas jacket with "Killer Catz Exterminator" embroidered on an appliqued roach.

Captain Verdi gestured toward the expanse of wall opposite the window. "This here's the spot," he said. Father Abrovaitas and Peppi walked to the center of the room and exchanged glances. Then Peppi stood back. The crowd assembled in rows facing the benches.

Father Abrovaitas scowled the group quiet, then cleared his throat. "We are here today to honor our mother, Lithuania, and her most noble son, Vytautas Lapidauskas, the artist of the picture we're about to unveil, which will hang forever in this place to commemorate the generosity and kind heart of our dear council . . ."

He waited until Mrs. Spassky quieted Acapulco, then bowed his head, saying, "Let us pray." There was a rustle in the crowd. "God who gave us Lithuania, bless this police station. May the peace and dignity of our homeland be bestowed on those who, for one reason or another, pass through. Amen."

"Now I turn to Mr. De Vencenzio," the priest said, stepping aside.

Peppi moved to the center. "I won't take long. I know everybody's waiting for Mrs. Retsina's refreshments." He pulled out a sheet of yellow tablet paper. "This is an important day in the history of the Southeastern Police Station because this is the day the Lithuanian people, folks who have given so much to America, so much to Baltimore, are to be honored by having this testimonial painting hanging here to remind them. Hey, Vito, come on up and show us the picture!"

Vito bounded next to Peppi, who gave him a quick hug, then watched while Vito tore the paper off the canvas and stepped back. "Come on, folks!" Peppi lifted Vito's arm over his head. "Let's hear it for Mr. Lapidauska!"

The crowd clapped. Captain Verdi nodded to a cop who pulled a molly bolt and drill from his pocket. He proceeded to set a nail in the cement block wall while the crowd fidgeted.

Peppi checked the back of the canvas and, with the cop's help, jockeyed the painting on the wall. Peppi stepped away and lifted his arms over his head, clapping. "One more time for the artist," he yelled above the applause. When the room quieted, he added, "I want to thank you all for coming out." He nodded to Father Abrovaitas. "To you, Father, for your beautiful sentiments." Captain Verdi and three cops staggered in with the loaded refreshment table. "Now for the iced tea," Peppi said, motioning everyone toward the table.

Galina started passing cheese and crackers while eyeing Vito in the center of the group around the picture.

"Like the old country."

"Prettiest trees I ever saw."

"Must have cost a fortune."

"I can't see God."

"Shut your damn trap."

Suddenly Galina overheard words that signaled her attention. Jay-Jay, holding a paper cup, was saying to Vito, "Sure is more of a future for you there than in Baltimore. Got people up there?"

"Can stay with Cousin George in Brooklyn 'til I find a place."

Galina stopped breathing. She had to steady herself against the table. He thinks his famousness is for real, she thought, so he's going to New York City. By the time she looked around again for Vito, he was showing Mrs. Spassky a frog in the painting.

The police station seemed empty when Mafalda and her kids left. Vito poured the last of the tea for a teenage boy with a suspended license while Galina gathered crumpled napkins and stuffed them into a trash can. "Got everything?" she asked, checking the benches.

Vito glanced at the dozing woman. "She slept through the biggest day of my life." He rummaged through the leftover food, pulled out a new box of crackers and set them beside the woman's shriveled hand. "Little bite for when she gets up," he said. "Did anyone want vodka?"

"Only Father Abrovaitas for his headache."

Vito heaved up the carton of leftovers and they strolled into the afternoon sun. Seagulls squawked, circling Jimmie the huckster, who rattled past, scales swinging from the back of his pickup. Galina wasn't able to wait until they got home. The words tumbled out. "You said something to Jay-Jay about George?" She couldn't see Vito's face behind the carton, but sensed him stiffen.

He answered into the cardboard. "I didn't know how to mention it." She heard him take a deep breath. "I have to go paint in New York for a while."

"Why?"

"To get thoroughly famous."

"What about your house?"

"Thought Nickolaidas Realty could handle it as rental until one way or the other. Taking train up tomorrow to look around, but I'll be back next week."

She stopped, turning to face him. "Pretty shabby, I think, that I had to hear you discussing things with strangers before with me, your best friend."

"I was afraid you'd be mad," he said, still walking.

She caught up with him. Words gathered in her mouth—careful, she warned herself. Break it gently that his famousness is phony. Stalling for time, she pretended to focus on the decorations in the neighbor's window. "Same stupid blue jay and choir boys Mrs. Trella puts up every spring," she said. She stopped in front of Mrs. Krepetsky's Pieta surrounded by plastic tulips. "Do you think this is tasteful?" she asked.

"You're mad at me," he said.

"Let me think."

As they came near his stoop, he thrust the carton into her arms. "Have last minute stuff to do before tomorrow."

He's tossing me away like salami skin, she fumed.

Later, with the television set muttering in the background, she realized she wasn't going to eat the cabbage roll she had heated and shoved it back in the refrigerator. She poured a jelly glass of vodka to kill the nerve, then went upstairs to bed.

From now on everything would be different. Tomorrow was Friday, but she wouldn't be dashing around buying this, cooking that. She felt lonely and Vito hadn't gone anywhere yet.

New York would be terrible for him, she reasoned. Spending his savings, no good soup; and all because I made up his life. I've got to make a clear breast of it first thing in the morning. Certainly he'll be glum but it will be best for him in the long run.

Her heart felt like a lead potato. She threw back the chenille spread and swung her legs over the edge of the bed. Should get it over with right now. She swung her feet back under the top sheet. Hold your horses, she thought. A minute later she kicked the sheet aside and jammed her feet into her rabbit slippers. Has to be done, she thought. She pulled her hair net off and slipped into her second-best dress, Vito's favorite shade of blue.

When she banged on his aluminum door, Queen Hedwig started to bark. Vito opened the door a crack. He was wearing the navy shirt, white tie, and pajama bottoms with a safety pin dangling from the drawstring. "What's wrong?" he asked, grabbing Queen Hedwig by the scruff of the neck as he opened the door. She marched past him into the living room and stood between his easel and card table covered with turpentine, linseed oil, and brushes soaking in orange juice cans.

"Nothing's wrong. Wanted to talk," she said.

He smiled. "I was on my way over to your place first thing tomorrow, but glad you're here." He looked so cheerful she decided to take her time before changing his life around again. He patted his hand over his hair, white and fine as a spider web. "I was in bed but couldn't sleep I was so wound up about this New York business. It's a second life for me, a new engine in a Model-T."

Guilt shot through her insides like pepper vodka.

"I'm flying," he said in an excited voice.

Then he looked down and nudged a pile of newspapers with his toe. "Thanks to you."

She looked up, startled.

"You were my heart," he said, thumping his chest. "Kept up my courage, picture after picture, even when I was sick and hungry . . ."

"When were you sick and hungry?"

"A manner of speaking."

She picked up a tube of cobalt blue and rolled up the bottom thinking, I came here to do what's best for him. Maybe best to keep my big mouth shut. Sure I could keep him in Baltimore by tearing down his castle I built. Only he's living in it now.

"You dropped in for special reason?"

She put the tube down. "I'll miss our Fridays."

"Tomorrow, I promised George I'd be there. But from now on, what's a four-hour train ride? I can catch the two o'clock every week and be here like usual at six."

"You'll be early," she said and laughed.

He walked over and put his arms around her. "You think I'd be forgetting about my heart?" he asked as she bumped her head against his sharp collar bone. She smelled Lucky Strikes and dog. "Hey," he said, "you're crying?"

She pulled a Kleenex from her sweater sleeve. "And how." She blew her nose.

He patted her head. "Everything's going to be the same, except different," he said.

Vito found clean glasses and some Pikesville

rye; then they toasted New York. It was three in the morning by the time she slipped out his door with Queen Hedwig on a harness and clothesline. "No trouble at all when you're gone," she'd assured Vito.

She strolled past the silent houses, listening to crickets in the dandelion spikes near the curb and to Queen Hedwig's nails tapping on the cement.

Funny thing, she thought, I feel more future coming with Vito going. Maybe he will be a great artist in New York. The one he's working on now, "The Duck Flies Over the Neiman," should bring a good price.

The street lamp glowed amber on the pavement. She looked down at her furry slippers on the sparkling mica and noticed kids had drawn a hopscotch grid on the walk. After a quick glance around, she hopped on blocks one and two, waited for Queen Hedwig to pad up beside her, then hopped on three and four. She looked up to be sure none of the lace curtains in the street windows were parted, then hopped on five, and stood on one foot—a Vilnius stork, waiting for a fish.

TWO

No Job Too Small

Maggie Zedonas parked beside the row of mailboxes and jumped from the cab of her Chevy pickup. There was nothing for her, but the flag was up on her parents' box. She eased Pops' *Catholic War Veterans News* and Ma's *Organic Medicine* from under the hornet's nest hanging like a pinecone from the inside roof. Back in the driver's seat, she tucked a strand of long blond hair behind her ear, then stepped on the gas. There was just enough time to drop off the mail before she and Jan went to the union picnic.

Pops' rooster, Chopin, marched across the road and Maggie tapped the horn. Ma, Pops, and the few families nearby had immigrated from Vilnius. Now they lived on what Maggie called the West Virginia Lithuanian Reservation, hanging together, suspicious, proud, eyeing their

23

Amerikanskus neighbors as if they were hawks circling the chickens. Maggie pulled up beside Pops' van with "Zedonas Home Improvements— No Job Too Small" stenciled on the side, and left her truck motor running. The porch boards creaked as she crossed to the screen and looked into the dark living room. "Anybody home? Stanny? Ma?" she called, pushing the door open.

As usual, Pops sat hunched over his World War II battleground—styrofoam cup mountains and a tinfoil Baltic Sea—set up on the kitchen table. Ma swung back and forth in the rocker, the only chair in the house strong enough to support her weight. Her left leg, wrapped in rags, was propped on a cement block. Pops waved, then went back to studying his toy general leading the Suwaulki Brigade across the Vistula. The rear troops were plastic Indians waving bows and arrows. "Woolworth's don't sell no Polish Cavalry," Pops had explained.

Ma squinted up from her knitting. A ball of pink yarn rested at her feet, and Maggie suspected she was making another poodle-dog whiskey bottle cover.

"Hey, Zedonas," Ma yelled. "Fix Maggie sandwich, piece of cake."

Maggie tossed the magazines on the counter top. "Never mind. I just came by to drop this off."

Ma stepped up the speed of the rocker with her good leg. "You hear what I hear at the Super-

Mart? Your husband, Mister Junkie, might be out on parole."

Maggie's stomach hardened into a gizzard. The room became still except for the whine of Number Ten Shaft of Pittsburgh and Weirton Industries (that everyone called PAW) a quarter of a mile away. "When?" Maggie asked.

"He don't write to you?" Ma asked.

Maggie bit her cuticle. "You know I told him not to." She winced and glanced down at the blood moon rising over her nail. She had been married to Randy for twelve years, and for ten he had been in jail. Twice he had been paroled and both times cops picked him up in Morgantown within a week on possession and sale. She took the napkin from under Pops' beer can to dab at her thumb when a crash came from the sun porch.

"Shit," Stanny hissed. His adult body swayed as his childlike fingers groped for the peas bouncing off his thighs onto the floor. The empty shelling pot rolled to a stop under the glider.

Ma craned her neck for a full view. "Keep those dirty hands off yourself," she yelled. Stanny's large head wobbled as he slid his palms from his lap to one on each knee. Maggie shifted her eyes to the begonias on the radiator. In the old country, women took care of the family. But Pops should put Ma's health above his notions of what men and women ought to do and help manage Stanny, all two hundred pounds of him needing to be fed, washed, and supervised. Ma held the bottle of homemade arthritis medicine up to the light and watched the peppercorns swirl, then settle to the bottom.

"Why won't you let me take you to Doc Spivik's?" Maggie asked. "He can give you something for the pain."

"He don't do no good but charge."

Maggie sighed and walked towards the door, stepping over Ma's hooked rugs that were scattered over the linoleum like placemats.

"And what if Mister Junkie finds his wife running around with Jan Sobieski?" Ma asked. Pops moved an Indian back an inch.

"I'll worry about that when I have to," Maggie said.

"Wait," Pops said. She turned with her hand on the screen hook. "I'll come by later to poke out that hornet's nest in your gutter."

Maggie thanked him, nodded goodbye, and ran across the porch to the truck. Coal chips sprayed from under her tires as she drove down the driveway to her house next door. The news about Randy made her panic, feel trapped. Marriage to get away from home had buried her in a mine with two shafts—divorce or adultery. She was tired of confessing to Father Casimer about Jan—she glanced at the stigmata on her thumb—and making more broken promises.

Home, she unlocked her kitchen door, checked the clock, then dashed into the yard to pull clean jeans off the line. Jan would be there in fifteen minutes.

An hour after the picnic was over she and Jan lay on a blanket on the grassy slope behind the playground. The night air smelled of honeysuckle. Slim green bugs treaded light under the white bulbs lighting the ballfield. The wind clacked the swings against their iron poles, and Maggie lay there thinking someday bones will be all that's left of me. Jan's weight pressed her to the grass. Love was not wrong. "Like this, it is," she heard Father say. She lifted her hips anyway as Jan tugged at her jeans. "Not here," she said.

"I don't want to leave tonight."

"Park in the lot behind the barn so Pops won't see your car."

Chopin crowed, and Maggie woke up. Jan's profile, etched against the dawn, was framed by the crisscross curtains. She leaned down to untangle a sheet from around her ankle when suddenly a shadow cut across the light. She turned to the window as a dark circle moved past the blind. She saw the spiky hair and brows, then Pops looking at her upside down. She pictured him lying on the roof cleaning the gutter. His head swung to the left, and she followed his line of sight to Jan, sprawled naked, crucified on the striped sheet. Then the head was gone.

"What time is it?" Jan mumbled.

She reached for the clock and decided not to

tell him about Pops. "Six," she said.

Jan ran his hand down her spine, "Damn bird forgot it's Sunday," he said.

She sat up and swung her legs over the side of the bed. "The Novena!" Her shoes were buried under the pile of their underwear. "I've got to drive the old people's bus to our Lady of Sorrows," she said, buttoning her blouse on her way to the stairs. "Only bad part of this job is working weekends. I'll heat the coffee."

Jan came into the kitchen and she held up the pot. "Want some?"

"I'll stop at Hardee's," he said. "I better beat it out of here before your old man gets up and decides to drop in." He put his arms around her. "Hey, Peanut, I'm to be on the picket line, PAW's bringing in scabs." She nodded against his chest. "I'll be over tomorrow night," he said softly.

The sound of Jan's Mustang turned into the hiss of simmering coffee. As Maggie stared into the pot, she sensed someone behind her. She turned and saw Pops standing in the doorway. Slowly he walked to the table and pulled out a chair. "Please, a cup for me, too."

A fly circled the bowl of peaches in the center of the table. She slid Pops a mug, keeping her eyes on the formica. Pops cleared his throat. "You are in a pickle," he said. Then added, "Like when General Podhorski had to decide whether to let his men live or die."

Nothing, she thought, means anything to

the old man except the war and his stories. She leaned towards him and said, "Only my problem is real."

"So was Podhorski's."

She slapped the table. "Once. Just once, why don't you pay attention to your family."

He tipped the spoon and watched the sugar trickle into the coffee. "Because it don't do no good. I build you kids this house so Randy might straighten up. He's still the same bum I told you not to marry."

Maggie walked to the window, pulled aside the curtain and gazed at the zucchini choking out the beans. "It wouldn't have mattered what Randy was. Anything to get away from Ma whining, you dumping Stanny on her—"

"He don't bother no one."

"His diapers bother Ma plenty."

"Men don't know about these things."

Her knuckles whitened around the curtain. "Aren't you lucky."

Pops banged down the mug, his jaw set. "A man's job is to give his kids bread and honor. But that was never enough for you." His gray eyes clouded. "In Vilnius, life was simple. Zedonas can't live in this country."

Maggie walked over and stood at his elbow.

"Zedonas is not an immigrant," he said quietly. "I am in exile."

As if touching a grounded hawk, she stroked his index finger, wondering what other parts of them were connected.

He held out his arm waist high. "Since you was that big, after Stanny, nothing I do was good enough for her. I buy candy, roast beef, still no good." He rose and carried the mug to the sink. "In this country mothers and fathers turn on each other." He shut off the spigot. "She turned you from me, too."

Maggie's throat tightened as he shuffled towards the door.

He paused and asked, "Got any squirt stuff for hornets?"

"Bottom cupboard."

He slipped out while she lifted the bus keys from the ring above the stove.

As soon as the old people were settled in their seats, Maggie backed the old school bus onto Second Street and headed towards the convent. She had just downshifted onto the highway when Vito, one of the passengers, leaned over her shoulder and said, "I think Mr. Kovak had an accident."

She parked on the shoulder and snapped on the hazard lights. Vito followed her down the aisle. "Wake up, Mr. Kovak," she shouted. His bright blue eyes focused on her hand patting the inside of his thigh. Good thing his daughter made special pants for him with wide legs, Maggie thought as she folded the trouser cuff over the urine bag strapped to his thigh. The smell of a creek behind an ancient village shot through the bus. Mrs. Stotsky peered over the back of her seat.

"Mind your business," Vito snapped.

"The connection leaked. The tape's loose, that's all," Maggie said. Mister Kovak frowned at the cobweb hairs stuck on a strip of surgical tape hanging from the catheter. His eyes filled with tears. "I have to go home?"

Vito cleared his throat. "He's been looking forward to this trip for weeks."

Maggie slipped the trouser leg back down. "We're not far from my place and I have adhesive tape."

She parked the bus beside her truck. There was something strange about the house; it was too quiet, she thought, unlocking the door. Then she remembered the hornets were gone.

The first thing she saw was Randy's embossed leather belt with a feathered roach clip on the buckle, draped over the bannister. Her mouth went dry. Instinctively, she glanced back to be sure Mr. Kovak still dozed with his head against the window, took a deep breath and headed into the kitchen.

Randy flipped his orange ponytail over his shoulder and waved. Her eyes narrowed. "Get your feet off the table."

He swung his cowboy boots to the floor and grinned. "That's one bad hello."

"How did you get in?"

He dangled a key on a paper clip. "I live here." He tossed it on the table and reached into the rolled up sleeve of his T-shirt for a pack of cigarettes. He shook one towards her.

31

"No thanks."

"I always said my old lady's one goddamn saint."

There was a new tatoo on his bicep. A naked woman, a sword up to the hilt between her legs, straddled the words, "Satan Lives."

"Get out," Maggie said.

Randy bounced on each foot as he paced the kitchen. "Tomorrow I'm going straight to Red Casey at PAW." Randy snapped his fingers. "He'll put me on just like that." The ice cube tray he reached for clattered to the floor. "Whooee," he yelled, scooping up cubes, pitching some in the sink and others in a glass.

"Are you doing speed?" she asked, knowing he'd never answer that.

"Then me and Blue Jay turn this shack into a autobody shop. Buy you a trailer to put upside the road." Randy smiled as he tapped an envelope of cherry Kool-Aid into the glass. "I'm home for good." He slid a paper bag across the counter top, pulled out a fifth of Mountaineer, filled the tumbler and held it out. "Sip?"

"You can't stay here."

His eyes widened. "We're lawful wedded."

She pushed past him to open the drawer under the counter. The adhesive tape lay beside a potholder. "I got a bus full of old people. When I get back I want you gone, hear me?"

He pulled down the window blind, then let go of the ring. The blind snapped up and spun around the top roller. "Hear me? Hear me?"

Randy shrieked, then laughed.

Maggie ran to the porch and leaned, shaking, against the bannister. Vito stuck his head out of the bus window and shouted, "Almost lunchtime."

"Hear me?" Randy's laugh drifted through the door.

She got into the bus and steadied herself by holding the back of each seat as she worked her way down the aisle. Crouching beside Mr. Kovak she began to peel off the wet tape while Vito tore new strips from the roll. "You look like a ghost, Magdalena. Smell make you sick?"

She checked that the urine bag was taped tight against the old man's thigh. "I'm okay."

A few minutes later, backing out of the driveway, she realized her hands felt numb. She glanced at her house. Crape myrtle branches scratched the fender as she turned onto Route Seven.

The convent was cool as a forest. Maggie knelt beside Vito and fingered the wooden rosary Ma brought from Vilnius and prayed to forget Randy's laughter. She prayed to have the peace of mind of Father Casimer, who strode the corridors like a grackle; for the serenity of Sister Hedwig, who glided past smug with grace.

Voices murmured in the next room and dishes clattered as the nuns wheeled in a lunch cart; the sound of swings clacking against iron poles.

Vito, the last to be dropped off, waved

goodbye. As Maggie lurched down the rutted track from his shack, she decided to forget trying to reason with Randy. If he was still in the house, she would spend the night with Ma. Tomorrow she could get a court order to throw him out.

The porch was dark, silent. Maggie snapped on a table lamp in the hall and walked into the living room. Randy was asleep on the sofa, his fingers brushing the newspaper Jan left on the floor yesterday. She walked quietly into the kitchen, so not to wake him, and set her purse on the counter beside the empty bottle of Mountaineer. The leather pouch Randy kept his pills in—drag bag he called it—was crumpled beside the bowl of peaches. Curious, she opened the drawstring and turned the bag upside down. One red capsule bounced off the counter onto the floor. Odd, Randy always carried at least fifty, she remembered.

Suddenly, everything seemed wrong. She ran into the living room and flipped on the overhead light. Randy's lips were blue. She knelt beside him and lifted his arm. It flopped to his side. "Randy, wake up!" She shook his shoulders until his eyelids flickered. He always took whiskey with downers to come off speed, she recalled, rubbing his wrists.

The front door slammed and Pops' voice floated from the hall. "Brought you slice of ham." He came into the living room. He set a platter on an end table and asked, "When did that bum get here?"

She looked up at Pops. "This morning. He came back to scab."

"Drunk?"

"On pills. And he finished a bottle."

Randy twitched, then his back arched and his body stiffened. Pops pushed her aside. "They swallow tongues," he yelled. He clamped Randy's jaw shut with the heel of his hand. Pops pulled a yellowed handkerchief from his back pocket. Randy's eyes flew open as Pops stuffed the cloth into his mouth.

"I'm calling the police ambulance," Maggie said, reaching for the phone on the credenza.

Pops jumped up and grabbed her shoulders. "No police in front of this house. There's been enough disgrace, you running around like some whore . . ."

He had never used that word around her before. "We can fight about Jan later," Maggie said, yanking his hands off her shoulders.

She started towards the phone again and Pops blocked her path. "Zedonas is in charge. I'll call Doc Spivik. You go stay with your mother." Sweat zigzagged down Pops' temples. Randy choked. Maggie lunged towards the sofa, and suddenly Pops whipped the back of his hand across her cheek. She staggered against the wall. "Get out," he yelled, pushing her to the door. Too surprised to resist, she found herself being shoved onto the porch. He slammed the door shut and she heard the lock click.

The breeze was warm and there was a white moon. Maggie stumbled across the yard, not caring where she ran. She crossed the path to Pops' house and turned up the hill into the orchard. Cicadas whirled in the branches. An owl heeled into the wind. Her blouse was sticking to her back and her chest was aching by the time she made it to the top of the ridge. She stopped and leaned against a gnarled apple tree. In the valley below, lights glowed in the windows above the post office and a spotlight shone on the coal pulley that rose from Number Seven Shaft and ended somewhere behind the trees.

The world was still in order, she realized. Only she was not. She slid down against the tree and sat on the grass Pops kept trimmed low as velvet between the trees. Her breathing slowed. In the morning she would call the police. When Randy was out of the hospital, if they took him there, he'd be sent back to the correctional house for breaking parole. Life would be back to normal. Except for the sin between her and Jan. She remembered Pops' words in the living room, the slap she deserved. He could forgive her marrying wrong, but not for Jan. She had made a mess of what Pops cared about most, his crazy notions of honor as a Zedonas, as a has-been Lithuanian gentleman, a soldier, maybe a man.

The apple tree leaves shone dark against the sky. In a few months they would be heavy with snow. It was time to end it with Jan, turn him into just a winter memory of August. She buried her head in her arms and did not look up until the lights in the valley had gone out.

The hill was steeper going down. The moon cast a shadow of branches over the words "No Job Too Small" on the van. Maggie crossed the yard, walking into the beam of light from the living room window. The front door was ajar; she closed it behind her.

"That you Magdalena?" Pops called.

She stood in the entrance to the living room. The sofa was empty, the newspapers piled on the seat. "Where's Randy?"

"Dead."

She shut her eyes so Pops wouldn't see the spurt of relief rupture her conscience. "What did Spivik say?"

His cigarette, its long ash about to drop, smoldered between Pops' thumb and fingers. "No doctor."

Suddenly the slap, Pops pushing her out the door, had new meaning.

"After that bum was finished I called the police medics," Pops said, then added, "to haul him away."

She and Pops faced each other, and she imagined a rope-ladder swinging between them. He gave me life twice, she thought. And made sure the gift was not asked for. Tears tightened her throat. "He wasn't worth your soul," she whispered.

He held his hands out, palms up. "You my

soul."

His lips hardened into chalk. "These hands have seen lots of blood. They busted one Nazi skull with a wrench on the dock in Gdansk. For years I kept that bastard's teeth in my pocket, twiddled them like dimes."

Maggie sank into the armchair across from Pops. "I never knew about the Nazi," she said, studying his face, wondering if he looked older than he had that morning, wondering if she would be able to rearrange her idea of him into a new formation as easily as he moved the cavalry across the kitchen table.

Pops struggled to his feet. "Zedonas finds Nazis here too." He nodded at the slice of ham. "You eat yet?"

All at once she felt free, released, like Ma's lace curtain sprung from its drying frame.

"Not yet."

He lifted the platter from the table. "I'll fix you a ham sandwich God would nibble."

She stared at the striped slipcover on the couch and listened to pots clang in the kitchen, then the hiss of frying meat. The smell of ham drifted into the room and suddenly she was hungry.

"Why's there no grated horseradish in this kitchen?" Pops yelled.

Maggie glanced at the ceiling and tried to think of a reason as she headed down the hall.

THREE

Society for the Benefit
of the Daughters of Vilnius

"Dumb Litvak woman," people say behind my back. Front or back my ears are in the same place.

Foreigners get used to the wisecracks, the pressure to act like everyone else. Sometimes I feel like a slab of dough being whacked at with a cookie cutter, scored quick, hard, to make my edges sharp. Outside the mold, the leftover me gets balled up and tossed in the garbage. Now it's one thing for America to be the Great Cutter. But when Mary Illonas tried to mold me, I had to slap that nemoksha back in her place. I bet if I had had more time between Vic Santoni's warning and the Daughters' meeting I could have saved the name of our club. As it turned out, I only got in one little lick.

The night of the Daughters of Vilnius meeting, Santoni's Best Baltimore Deli was running a special on Spirits of Maryland rye. I picked up a bottle just in case Ruthie, the refreshment committee, ran out. Vic Santoni was leaning on the counter watching old Mr. Ambrosius, whose parrot-toe fingers were curled over the edge of the bread bin. The old man reached out and poked at a loaf.

"You want one or don't you?" Vic asked.

"Hard as baseball bat," Ambrosius muttered.

Glad Vic's too busy to kid around I thought, watching him shake his finger at the old man. "Nickko pulls it from the oven every hour on the dot," Vic shouted.

"When's next load?"

Vic scowled at the clock. "Eight."

Ambrosius sat on a codfish crate and crossed his legs. We Lithuanians are stubborn as grease stains.

Vic snorted at the old man, then turned and spotted me standing beside the freezer. "What's for you today, Mrs. Kalaikas?"

"Got my four dozen poppyseeders?"

He rummaged under the counter. "Need anything else for the meeting tonight?"

"What did Ruthie buy?"

"Five pounds of Binkas sausage, prefried."

I slid the rye across the counter.

Vic looked up from biting the string on the bakery box and pointed to a sign taped to the cash register. "Read that!" he ordered.

My throat turned into a lead pipe. Although

I talk blue streaks in American, I never learned
to read or write in English. I ducked my head
towards my shopping bag and pretended to look
for something. "What?" I asked as if I hadn't
been listening.

He held up the bottle. "Have to be twenty-
one to drink this stuff."

My throat loosened up. "You're pretty
funny," I said. "You should go on the television.
You know I'm better than forty-one."

The knot on his throat went up and down.

"Hear that Ambrosius? She says she's better
than forty-one." While he counted the change
into my hand I studied the provolones that
swung like wrecking balls on ropes from the
ceiling. Something different hit my palm and I
looked down at a piece of halvah. Vic whistled at
Ambrosius. "Catch," he yelled tossing another
piece. The old man grabbed it and grinned, his
mouth empty as a Sunday warehouse loading
dock.

"What's the occasion?" I asked.

"I have to treat big shots."

"Who big shots?"

He rolled his eyes. "I happen to know Mary
Illonas is naming you secretary of the Daughters
tonight. The way you Polacks are taking over the
world," Vice raised his fist, "next thing I know
you'll be the Mayor's right hand."

When he said Polack, I winced, but figured
his type weren't smart enough to figure out
Lithuanians came from a different country even

41

if I told him the difference. "Hey, just because our secretary Josie moved to Detroit I don't think Mary would name me. What makes you so sure?"

"Ruthie."

I pictured Ruthie's two hundred pounds bouncing across Vic's wooden floor, heels click-clicking on the patent leather tap shoes she always wore. Ruthie, bending Vic's ear, fooling with her pink satin hair band, her elbows like truck tires as she leaned over the counter.

Was I on the hot spot. The Daughters' business was conducted in English. I'd have to speak up in front of everyone that I don't read or write. I turned away from Vic and backed towards Mr. Ambrosius. "Meeting's in half hour," I said, trying to act as if nothing was wrong.

"Ciao, Madam Secretary," Vic said. I jangled the door shut.

I stepped into the gummy August twilight and rolled up my flight jacket sleeves. It was hot as an asbestos bathrobe, but it had the awards my kid Johnny got in Viet Nam sewn on. I stood beside a hydrant painted with a crab scuttling over some words and waited for the light to change.

When I was eighteen, I should have studied English for foreigners as soon as I got off the flight from Vilnius. I suppose everyone else in the world is perfect? At that time my life was exploding like ice water hitting a hot skillet. I got the job as hostess at Stan's Bar of Distinction. Then was Mrs. Stan Kalaikas. Then Johnny. Then Vito. I parked the bassinets behind the beer cooler while I wiped the counters.

My Stan always says, "Smart girls stay dumb and play dumb." So I kept my mouth shut about not reading. I guess everyone figured I read *The Southeast Baltimore World Opinion* every morning. Maybe they think I read books? Who knows. But if I spilled the beans now, it would look like I had been putting wool on people's eyes for years. I checked my reflection in the Kopernik Bank window and pulled in my stomach. Best thing, I decided, rounding the corner to Saint Casimer's side door, would be to say thank you, Madam President, but Stan and I are opening a subsidiary and will be busy around the clock. Good thing Vic warned me. I pushed the church door open.

Lysol and Sunday school crayon smells hit me, then sneaker smells when I passed the locker room. Not like Saint Isidore's in Vilnius; wet wool, and hair tonic that smelled like steam from boiling gardenias.

The gym was set with rows of chairs from Skardas' Funeral Home, with English words stenciled on the back. Up front was a folding table where Father Abrovaitas, President Mary, Treasurer Rose, and Secretary Whoever would preside. These meetings reminded me how slapped together I felt. I bet the others felt it too. As if we were Kaunas cottages sided with NU-LOOK or Baltic amber set in plastic. Our roots were no longer in the peat bogs of Anykščiai. But they weren't exactly cemented in George Washington's tomb, either. We were in-between-countries people; only ourselves with each other. That's why the Daughters club was special.

Ruthie waddled around the card table. "Plunk them rolls next to the sausage," she said. I set the poppyseeders beside Daughter punch: pineapple juice and rye, Ruthie's American version of virytus which in the old country is rye, kummel seeds and lemon.

I looked around for someone to chat with. Not only Ruthie, but everyone else seemed busy. Elena was creasing the folds of the Maryland, Baltimore, and United States flags. Tillie was carrying a centerpiece of plastic flowers stuck in the hat of a ceramic Mexican. I chose a folding chair up front and sat down as Father swooped in beside Mary. Right away she stomped over to check Ruthie's setup the way General Pilsudski would inspect wormy troop meat. The gym started to fill up with Daughters, some husbands who had to drive and decided to stay in the conditioning, and a few little kids.

"Like an oven outside."

"How long this thing supposed to last?"

Ruthie wiggled down beside me just as Mary tapped her water glass with a pen. "Welcome to the two hundred first meeting of the

Society for the Benefit of the Daughters of Vilnius," she announced.

Ruthie leaned close to me. "Mary's new permanent looks like a pumpkin," she giggled.

Mary shot a frown in our direction. "There will be a short meeting tonight because of the Orioles game." She turned to the priest who beamed up at her. "Father?"

I inched off my zorrie sandals and got ready for the long haul. Father would order us to serve God, Lithuania, America, and Saint Casimer's in a different lineup each meeting. We'd salute the flag, then wait while Mary found her pitch pipe to get us going on the "Star Spangled Banner," "God Bless America," and "Maryland, My Maryland." We had to pretend we were born here Americans so no one could see we weren't. I used to polish the windows of our row house every day because people thought foreigners were dirty. If the windows were clean no one could tell who was inside.

Rose droned on with the minutes and treasurer's report. "Finally," she whined, "we took in five hundred twenty-two from the July bake sale."

Mary thanked Rose, then glared over her glasses at Ruthie. "Not naming names you understand, but Father got complaints about stale babka from the City Hall booth." She cleared her throat. "To the wise, that's all."

Then Mary hunched forward like a hawk on a telephone pole. "The next business is our joining the Maryland Federation of Women's Organizations. As you recall, back around the holidays Jane Whittier," Mary paused "of Whittier Shipping, and chairlady of the AFWO called me up personally to ask if the Daughters would consider becoming a dues-paying affiliate. I remind you, each of us will get a newsletter with colored pictures and we'll send a delegate to the annual meeting at the Hilton Hotel."

I remembered Mary mentioning the idea, but like most of her fancy plans, I figured it would bomb.

Mary nodded to Rose and Father. "The executive committee sent a letter saying how pleased we were to join." I sat straighter. She held up a piece of paper. "This lovely letter came welcoming us as their newest member group."

How much pushing and pulling, I wondered, had it taken to get Father and Rose to go along? Not much, I figured looking at Father's oily grin, Rose's blush.

"Only one more technicality," she went on. "I was worried that our name would look funny in the list of affiliates on the newsletter cover. To change it, our accountant says we need an official vote." Her eyes swept the room. "So do I hear a motion to change our name from 'The Society for the Benefit of the Daughters of Vilnius' to 'The Southeastern Baltimore Women's Club'?"

I felt my neck flare like a match hitting kerosene.

Someone from behind piped up, "Who thought up the new name?"

Mary looked at Father. He smiled wider, flashing a graphite tooth. "New name sounds more refined for you nice ladies."

We sounded refined enough when we raised two grand to fix his rectory furnace, I thought. I glanced at Ruthie whose blue eyes were getting as shiny as her taffeta dress. I patted her knee. "Don't cry," I whispered.

Suddenly Judy Baylas, a nice kid, Tillie's granddaughter, stood up in the first row. "If we change our name we won't be an official Lithuanian club anymore, just another women's group raising money to float a central office on Charles Street."

First I was surprised. Then I figured it out: Judy was young and the kids seemed to be looking for roots these days. Folk songs, natural hair, homemade bread.

"Everything will be the same," Mary said, cool as a scallion. "We'll just be swimming in the mainstream, that's all."

"Drowning," Judy muttered.

Ruthie leaned again and hissed in my ear. "Mary just wants to hang out in the Hilton with Mrs. Whittier and talk about stale babka."

"Why don't you say something?" I whispered back.

"I'm scared of her."

I couldn't stand up because my zorrie was lost under a seat. "Mrs. Illonas," I began. "Most of us, except daughters of Daughters," I waved at Judy who turned to face me, "come from the old country. Although we're Americans first, we feel better keeping our Lithuanian habits. We owe it to our young people not to lose our name in the scuffle. Why not hang on to it and still hook with the AFWO?"

"Why not?" echoed Ruthie.

"Why not shove the AFWO and their damn colored pictures," Judy yelled.

Father winced and Mary banged the glass even though the room was quiet. "Do I hear a motion?" she barked.

I remembered Elena with the flags and realized Mary had lined up the members. I could hear her telling them we would be big shots now.

Old Tillie Baylas hung her cane on the back of a chair and stood, ivory cardigan swinging from her bony shoulders. "New name is best," she said. "We must be prideful these important people want us, thanks to the hard work of Mary Illonas, our president."

Mary looked relieved. "Second?"

"I do," mumbled ancient Francina.

The old ones sell out, I thought.

"All those in favor?"

Hands flapped up like pigeons in front of the huckster. My arm was ready to fly on "opposed" and I felt Ruthie's shoulder tense, but Mary whacked the table with her pen and said, "Unanimous!" She took off her glasses, wiped them with her hanky and settled the rhinestone

rims back on her nose. "The last item of business is the naming of our new secretary. To
replace Josie, I am appointing Mrs. Valiute
Kalaikas, who, as you recall, carried the ball on
the living nativity and the bus trip to Atlantic
City." A few Daughters clapped.

I was so mad about the name change I
hardly heard Mary's words. The old people had
sold out, but good. The way a lot of immigrants
did when they changed their names on Ellis
Island, or moved into Protestant neighborhoods,
or learned how to cook meatloaf. I wanted to be
American too, but not that bad. All the old
timers had cared about was finding jobs, buying
real estate, and putting their kids through
college.

Then it hit me they hadn't been so dumb
after all. They had enough sense to realize
America was a good place, and guts enough to
change. Young people should understand how
tough that was. All at once I wasn't mad anymore. Maybe the older Daughters just forgot to
remember heritage is a tree for kids to swing
from and chopped it down by mistake. I'll bet
Tillie never realized how Judy would feel with
no branches to climb, no roots. The old people
were too careless, but the kids were too critical.
So where did that leave the in-betweeners like
me?

"Valiute?" Mary smiled.

It was time for my speech about Stan and
the subsidiary. My foot found my zorrie under

Ruthie's chair and I slipped it on. Meanwhile my head was going around and around.

"Stand up," Ruthie whispered.

I struggled to my feet. "Thank you for this honor." My voice sounded faint. I squared my shoulders so my hands would stop shaking. "I will be proud to serve as secretary of the South-eastern Baltimore Women's Club," I said, louder. "And I'll try to be as regular as Josie with the minutes." Suddenly I lost my nerve, started to sit, then straightened. "By the way, it just so happens I don't read or write English so I'll be doing Daughter business in Lithuanian. First thing, I'll write to thank Mrs. Whittier." I sat down fast and held my breath, waiting for the lightning to hit.

The room was quiet except for a dull clicking sound. I looked up and saw Father cracking his knuckles, one by one. Mary's lips were a straight line. Ruthie coughed, her hand over her mouth and I could tell from her eyes she was trying hard not to laugh.

"When's refreshments?" a husband asked.

Mary tapped her water glass. "Meeting is adjourned. Rose will call you personally about bake sale drop off points." The scrape of chairs drowned her voice. I stood, stretched, then lifted my jacket from the back of the chair.

"You're a real wise guy," Ruthie said. "Only next thing, Mary's going to try to bump you off as secretary."

Ruthie was right. "Just let her try," I said. I

sounded braver than I felt. "Maybe you and I can help the younger Daughters fight back."

Ruthie nodded. "We must hang onto what was beautiful in the old life. Kugelis . . ." Ruthie went on while I slipped towards the door.

Halfway across the room someone touched my elbow. I turned to face Judy Baylas who held out a styrofoam cup. I took the punch and she touched the rim of hers to mine.

"Sveikas, Aunt Valiute," she said.

FOUR

Anchovy Trees

Dinner was included in Franklin Taken-Alive's rent. But when Hedy Petrosky served kielbasa or cabbage rolls, the old Sioux only picked. She liked to fix him corn pudding or chokeberry stew, to cheer him up. He leaned forward and rubbed his hand across his silver and turquoise belt buckle. "Your fry-bread's looking better," he said.

Hedy untangled a strand of her graying blonde hair from her earring. "Eat. The mister should be along any minute."

Taken-Alive had moved into the attic of the Petrosky's Baltimore row house a year ago after his apartment building had been condemned. Hedy gathered he left the Pine Ridge Reservation and had come to work at Sparrow's Point Steel. Now, pensioned, he spent his days sitting on the marble stoop, his ballpoint eyes marking the comings and goings of Baylis Street. Nothing slipped past him. Hedy sensed he was even aware of her latest worry over her husband Cash.

Every night after work Cash strode past Taken-Alive on the stoop and bounded up the marble steps next door, where Bora Slovonjak lived. She was pushy, that one. First off, when she moved in she had knocked on Hedy's back door and asked to borrow a hammer. Cash insisted on nailing up the curtain-rod fixtures for their new neighbor. Next thing Hedy knew, he was fixing Bora's rotten porch railings. "After all, I'm a carpenter," he reminded Hedy. "Then why not charge?" she asked.

Cash spent weeks building Bora a bookcase, answering Hedy's complaints with clenched teeth and silence. When first married, twenty years ago, Cash and Hedy could talk, kid around. The years had smothered his humor like a furry gray mold.

Taken-Alive tore a piece of fry-bread in half. "How's the bookcase coming along?"

"Finished." Hedy slid the jar of honey towards him. "But Cash dropped by Bora's after work and found out her fuse box was busted. He came in to change clothes, then said he'd be back soon as her electric's on."

The sound of spiked workboots clicked across the porch, and Hedy paused with her hand on the back of a chair. Cash stepped into the kitchen and the herbal smell of wood shavings filled the room. She looked up at his tanned jaw and the lean muscles under his polo shirt and as usual, her breath quickened.

"I said come on in," Cash called over his shoulder.

Bora leaned in the doorway, one hand on the frame, the other in the hip pocket of her jeans. "I'm barging, as usual, but Cash said was all right."

Hedy eyed her neighbor's tumbling black curls streaked with gray, teeth white against plum lipstick, and felt dowdy — a skinny housewife wearing her husband's old shirt.

"This little lady's got no electric," Cash said. "I guess we can rustle up some dinner for her." Hedy forced a smile and tied an apron over her slacks. Cash jabbed Bora's arm with his elbow. "Over there's Franklin Taken-Alive. Bet you seen him on our stoop."

The Indian's eyes narrowed and Bora shrugged. Cash opened the refrigerator and yelled, "Who's for firewater?"

Taken-Alive clenched his fist, and quickly Hedy reached around Cash, pulled out two Budweisers, and set one in front of the old man. A minute later Cash was leaning over Bora and pouring her beer into a tall glass.

"You Hungarian?" Hedy asked.

Bora's green eyes widened. "I'm from Yugoslavia." She slid a gold horse back and forth along a chain around her neck.

"Then you must know the Rabovics," Hedy said.

Bora laughed. "Came to the States last month from Canada. No work up there."

Probably some gypsy, Hedy thought. "What do you do?" she asked.

Bora set down her glass and wiped her mouth on the sleeve of her plaid shirt. "Hostess, waitress, whatever."

"There should be no problem," Hedy said, ladling barley into a bowl, "finding work like that in Baltimore."

Bora sighed. "Not if I was here legal with green card."

Cash held a loaded serving spoon over Bora's plate. "She's got visa problems up to her neck. Political in the old country, then some brush with the Toronto cops."

"You mean bust-up for hash," Bora laughed.

Cash reddened and glanced at Taken-Alive.

"You don't seem worried to mention dope," Hedy said.

"Why should I be scared to mention anything?" Bora held up her empty glass. "What's done is done."

While Cash and Bora ate, Hedy sat beside Taken-Alive and eased off her sandals. Cash shoved a shank bone to the edge of his plate and said, "I think our company's ready for coffee," then added, "And some of that fancy whiskey on the top shelf."

Hedy stood on tiptoe to reach the brandy while Bora, leaning close to Cash, swung the gold horse in small circles. Something she said made him laugh.

Damn Cash has always been inconsiderate,

Hedy thought. When Joe, their only kid, was born, Cash took off for Seattle. "To get my head straight," as he put it. A month later he came back homesick and broke. Hedy took in the neighbor's kids a few hours a day until he got on his feet.

Last summer he cleaned out their savings account and bought an antique Packard. "It's a classic," he explained the day before he smashed it up on the beltway. Hedy was replacing the account with Taken-Alive's rent money. As a child in Warsaw, Hedy learned that eventually someone tore down or blew up whatever you built. Life was a matter of renovating, that's all.

Bora leaned across the table to light Taken-Alive's cigarette and the lighter dropped into the ashtray. "Whoops," she yelled, then laughed and drained her third brandy. "Time for this little Bora to go home," she said, struggling to her feet. "I thank you for—"

"No trouble," Hedy said.

Cash kept his hand on Bora's elbow as she tottered to the screen door. "Don't worry, I'm right behind you," he said, as she stepped onto the porch.

He started out the door and Hedy grabbed the back of his shirt. "Where are you off to?"

"Help her home," Cash said.

"To next door?"

Cash faced her. "Don't tailgate me."

"You come right back."

"As a matter of fact," he said slowly, "I might come back tonight." He turned. "Or I might not," he said over his shoulder and slammed the door.

Bora's giggle, drifting through the screen, filled the room like the smell of burning lard.

Hedy stared into the back yard. Taken-Alive came up beside her, shadows turning his face into an icon. "Did you hear?" she asked.

He nodded. His shoulder length hair, clasped with a silver barrette at the nape of his neck, gleamed like wet feathers.

"Why would God let some woman destroy my home?" Hedy whispered.

Taken-Alive picked up his cigarettes. "So you could rebuild it." He moved towards the doorway. "Get some sleep."

Hedy knew these things happened; she wasn't born yesterday. Only they happened to people like the no-account Stotleys, to movie stars, to French people.

She roamed around the kitchen, then lay down on the daybed in the living room. A minute later, she was prowling the hall, then standing at the front door. The marble stoop gleamed like an altar in the glow from the streetlight. Smells of creosote and fish drifted from the harbor. Suddenly, she spotted waffle-prints from Cash's boots on her clean steps. She bent, ran her finger over a heel mark and sniffed. Sure enough, oil.

Hedy grabbed a bucket from the broom closet. Steam billowed as she filled the pail with water and ammonia. With the bucket in one hand and a can of lye in the other, she headed towards the stoop. The fumes made her gag as she knelt and dipped the brush into the water, but the lye did the trick on the footprints. A dandelion had sprouted between the steps and the sidewalk and after yanking it out, she doused the crack with more lye. Now, there were mud streaks on the cement that needed to be scrubbed off.

A squad car slowed along the curb and she squinted into the headlights. Mario Russo leaned out the window. "You okay Mrs. Petrosky?" She waved.

"Why are you scrubbing the sidewalk?" he shouted.

She shook out the brush. "Getting rid of some dirt before it sets."

He watched her for a minute, then gunned the motor and drove off. She knelt staring at the rag, an old T-shirt soft as wet bread. Slowly, she looked up at Bora's living room window, at the peeling frame and closed blinds. The bedroom windows were dark too. The streetlight reflected the glass that was rain-scarred as if tears had run down from the roof.

She smelled leather, then a sudden weight fell across her shoulders and she looked up at Taken-Alive, who held the hem of a buffalo robe. "Stand up," he said.

"I don't think I can," she whispered. Then his hands were under her arms and she was on her feet. Her fingertips were puckered and the skin was swollen over her wedding ring. Although it made her sweat, she clutched the robe around her as she walked into the house,

Taken-Alive beside her.

The mantel clock struck one as she lay down on the daybed. Taken-Alive flipped the robe over her feet, then disappeared. Circles of moonlight shone through the lace curtains. Her hands smelled like lye. Eyes burning, she wondered if she would ever sleep again. The floorboards squeaked, then Taken-Alive was looming over her.

"Take this," he said.

Propped on one elbow, she took the glass of water he offered and studied the white capsule he held in his palm.

"What is it?"

"Something for the pain."

When she awoke, sun dappled the beige carpet. Smells of coffee came from the hall. The refrigerator door slammed and Cash whistled in the kitchen. The misery of last night took up where it left off.

Cash was buttering a bagel, his eyes pimento red and his chin bristling with ashy stubble. A knight appliqued on the breast pocket of his polo shirt hung by a thread. Hedy walked to the stove and tipped the coffee pot.

He jumped up and said, "I'll fix more."

She waited until he turned off the water tap. "Where were you?"

He held the pot midair. "I got to take it from the beginning." He opened the cupboard, lifted out a can of coffee, then rummaged in the drawer.

"Can opener's on the counter," she said.

He cleared his throat. "Bora's cousin's giving her a job in Ohio." He added, "She needs me to go with her."

Something inside Hedy disconnected, causing her stomach to float. "When? Where in Ohio?"

"Don't give me no third degree," he snapped. His hands trembled as he filled the sieve.

Anger hit her like heat when she opened the oven. "You got responsibilities."

"Joe's in the Navy."

"So I'm in the garbage?"

He snapped on the burner. "I'll send money regular."

She glanced up at the statue of Our Lady of Perpetual Sorrow on the ledge over the sink. Every week Cash slipped his paycheck under its ceramic base. "What happened," she asked softly, "to make you run with that tramp?"

"Nothing happened. I just want a new life."

Hedy's eyes burned. "What's the matter with the one you got?"

He picked at the knight on his shirt.

The marble swirls in the linoleum blurred. "I feel sick," she whispered.

He slammed his fist on the asbestos pad. "Don't make it no harder for me," he shouted.

"You're like some animal that dirties its nest," she said. Her face felt hot. Calm down, she thought. The ashtray Bora had used was on the counter and Hedy walked over and emptied it. Butts smeared with lipstick leered at her from inside the garbage bag. "I'm taking out the trash," she said. As she pushed past him on the way to the door, he dropped the knight on the counter.

In the yard, a mourning dove cooed from a telephone wire. She strode along the phalanx of hollyhocks along the alley. Turning the corner onto Baylis Street brought her to the front of her row house. She dropped the green plastic bag of garbage into the can. The old Indian sat at his post. She checked the lid to make sure it was on tight, then walked over to Taken-Alive, who shielded his eyes from the sun. "Cash is leaving," she blurted out.

Taken-Alive tapped his cigarette ash into the potted geranium on the stoop. "He'll come back."

"Fifty years old and that gypsy made up his mind."

"That's the age a man learns he's grown as tall as he'll ever grow."

Hedy bent to pick a shriveled blossom off the stem. "Cash knew his limits until she gave him high ideas."

"You don't look so hot. Had breakfast?"

She shook her head and he flipped the butt into the street and stood. "Come on."

As she trotted to keep up with him, she drew a circle around her ear. "You ever see a nut like that Bora?"

"Not in South Dakota."

Mario Russo blew the horn and waved as he cruised past in the squad car. Hedy stopped and grabbed Taken-Alive's arm. "Suppose I was to turn her in to immigration?"

The Indian's profile seemed to sharpen.

"Bora said she was here illegal. No green card."

Taken-Alive resumed walking, only slower. "Do they always send your people home? Or would she just get a smart lawyer?" he asked.

Hedy's voice was harsh with excitement. "Immigration shipped Veronica Spassky back to Prague after her ex ratted. Nothing her lawyer could do about it."

Taken-Alive pushed open the glass door of Mafalda's Pizza Paradise and motioned for Hedy to choose a stool. Hedy, picturing Bora wearing handcuffs and boarding a plane, smiled and reached for a menu.

Tony De Vencenzio wiped his tomato-stained hands on a towel hanging from his belt. "What's your poison?"

Taken-Alive held up two fingers. "Anchovy pizzas and root-beers."

"Anchovies?" Hedy raised her eyebrows. "You said you can't eat fish."

Taken-Alive gazed into the mirror over the grill and smoothed the hair over his ears.

"You said," Hedy added, "that it was against your—"

"Anchovies grow on trees in the Black Hills," he said.

Tony slammed down a platter of pizza, then dove into the back room. Taken-Alive stared at the molten tomato sauce as if it held the right words. "If you were my daughter, I'd tell you to lay off this immigration business."

Hedy blew on a forkful of mozzarella. "It's my only chance with Cash," she said.

"To do what?" he asked. "Keep your hide wrapped around his tent pole?"

She folded her pizza and bit off the tip. "He's my life," she said.

"Make your own. You mentioned you were a nurse in Poland?"

She shrugged. "Years ago. I came to America when I was twenty-one. No future in Warsaw."

He mopped up the sauce with a piece of crust. "Same reason I left Pine Ridge," he said. "Maybe when a person comes from a place that's being kicked around they get used to being kicked around themselves."

She nodded. "From time to time I think about going back to work" She pushed aside her plate and sighed. "Who would ever hire an unlicensed nurse who hasn't practiced in over twenty years?"

Taken-Alive laughed as he picked up the check. "The Indian Health Service."

Strolling towards the house, Hedy thought up arguments to stall Cash. She thanked Taken-Alive on the stoop, squared her shoulders, and headed through the dining room.

A note was propped on the napkin holder. She froze, her thoughts jumbled. Cash couldn't have gone so soon. What about the bowling tournament? She grabbed the sheet of tablet paper and read aloud, "The electric's still off. Took the camper up Middle River. Be back Sunday. Don't worry about the Coleman lamp." She lifted her head. The knight lay on the counter, its French knot eye staring at the crack on the ceiling.

That afternoon she painted the kitchen chairs yellow. Taken-Alive ate dinner alone, while she unclogged leaves from the gutter with a rake handle. At midnight, the thought of the desolate bedroom drove her to put sheets on the daybed. As the clock struck two, she was imagining Cash and Bora on the bunk in the camper. Her insides were shredded flesh, as if the machinery that pumped, soothed, and digested had been torn out. At three, her face still clammy against the pillow, she recalled Taken-Alive's pills. She shoved her feet into tennis shoes and headed upstairs.

Snores floated through his door. She paused, then remembered he didn't have to get up in the morning. "Mr. Alive," she called. "You got a minute?"

Shuffling; then he opened the door. He wore a gray jogging suit with maroon stripes down the sides. His hair swung loose. "What's wrong?"

"I can't sleep and wondered if that pill—?"

He motioned her to wait. A drawer slammed, then he returned carrying a three pound coffee can. He peeled back the plastic lid and tipped the can towards her.

"What are they?" she asked.

"Snowflakes."

"Where did you get them?" she asked. He put his finger against his lips. "Thank you very much," she said, as if accepting a dinner mint.

"Goodnight," he yawned. His door clicked shut. Before she got to the bottom step, the idea assembled. She turned on one foot, ran back, and banged on his door. He opened it.

"Sell me those," she said.

He leaned forward and grabbed her shoulder. "Put that out of your head."

"Not for me," she snapped. "I'll plant them on the gypsy tomorrow night before I go to immigration."

He shook his head. "That's getting in too deep."

She tightened the cord on her bathrobe. "When you mentioned the lawyer, I got to worrying. To be sure Bora gets kicked out, I need for them to know she's a criminal."

"How do the flakes get on her?"

Hedy thought out the details as she spoke. "Bora's place is built like ours. You know that hatchway by the rosebush?"

He nodded.

"It goes to the cellar. Bet she has a padlock on hers, too. I'll bust the lock."

Taken-Alive smacked his palm against his head. "You're no second-story man. Messing with immigration is one thing but breaking and entering's another. You'll be tossed in jail."

Her eyes widened. "I don't believe Mario Russo would ever do that."

He held up his palm. "A belief is the flower

of a wish," he said.

She grinned. "Anchovy trees?"

He rubbed his ankle with his other foot.

"How much do you want for the flakes?" she asked.

"Friends don't sell to each other. I'll give you some on condition—"

"No way—"

"That you sleep on this nonsense. If you still have the stomach for it in the morning, I'll go with you. I want to see where those pills wind up."

"You don't trust me."

"You, but not your crazy ideas." He started to close the door. "Besides, nice ladies don't know how to saw off locks."

Her throat tightened. "Thanks," she said.

The next night, Hedy was tying on a plastic raincap patterned with ducks just as Taken-Alive lumbered into the kitchen. His black nylon shirt stretched over a pack of cigarettes in his breast pocket. A woven headband, knotted at the nape of his neck, circled his forehead; a few eagle feathers on the ends hung over his shoulder. "It's not too late to change your mind," he said.

"It won't take but a minute."

He sighed and handed her a plastic bag full of the pills. "I'll need a flashlight and a hacksaw," he said.

Hedy pulled a key from her apron pocket. "The mister took the Coleman. But get what you need from the shed out back."

A few minutes later, Taken-Alive burst into the kitchen, stomping his boots on the doormat. "It's pouring buckets."

"I'll get us an umbrella."

"It would slow things down. Come on, let's get this over with."

She pulled on a raincoat, jammed the pills into her pocket, and followed him. Rain dripped from the cap on to her eyebrows. Stumbling, she almost knocked over a bird bath the last tenants left in Bora's yard. The cellar hatch loomed before them like a sloping casket. Taken-Alive squatted beside the padlock. "Shine the flashlight on my hands," he said. Rain polished his thumbnail as he drew the saw back and forth. He handed her the lock. "Stand back while I open the door."

A moldy smell shot through the rain. Hedy looked at the crumbling cement steps. "You go first," she said.

They crept into the cellar, then picked their way around pyramids of paint cans and broken garden tools. Taken-Alive pushed aside a rusty lawn mower, and Hedy shone the light on the door to the first floor.

She followed him up the stairs and into the kitchen, focusing a beam on the chrome toaster that gleamed like a three-quarter moon. "Don't waste time," he snapped. "Where does the stuff go?"

"Somewhere in with her clothes," Hedy said, trailing him through the living room.

"Hand me the flashlight," he ordered, and

mounted the steps.

Suddenly, a voice from a bedroom screamed, "Vodka!"

"Vodka, Vodka." Followed by a squawk.

Taken-Alive paused in the hall. "A bird," he said, then walked towards the bedroom. As he crossed the threshold, there was a clank and a shuffle.

"What did you step on?" she asked.

He stooped and lifted a yard-long chain. She raised her head and watched the cone of light play around the room. She saw a six-foot high rattan cage with pillows on the floor. A smaller cage bounced from an arched hanger bolted to the doorframe. Inside, a black bird bobbed its head over a plastic cup. "A myna," Hedy whispered.

Taken-Alive swung the light on to an enlarged photograph on the wall of Bora peering from between the legs of a gorilla. The light skimmed a mattress on the floor. Instead of a spread, the bed was covered with waxed paper. A velour tiger-skin afghan lay folded at the foot. Taken-Alive focused on a swastika painted on a sheet hanging from the ceiling. He snapped off the flashlight. Hedy reached for it. "You've seen enough," he said.

She stumbled to the window and yanked open the velvet drapes. A plastic bowl on the windowsill almost fell. When she grabbed it, she noticed the incense holder in its center. The streetlight shone on more wall photographs she couldn't make out. Aside from the mattress and cage, the only furniture was a nightstand with bottles crowded on top. Hedy lifted a jar labeled "Passion Lotion."

The wax paper crinkled, as Taken-Alive sat cross-legged on the bed. He took out his cigarettes and nodded at the swastika. "Your people have strange beliefs."

Suddenly she thought of Warsaw: the faded posters with German slogans plastered to the wall under the Poniatowski Bridge. One depicted a Nazi boot crushing an American flag. Another showed the Polish falcon in flames. One evening, when no one was around, she tore down the poster of an Aryan princess gazing up at a soldier on a horse. She ripped off a corner and slipped it into her shoe over the hole in the instep. Later, she leaned over the railing of the bridge and dropped the remaining pieces into the glossy Vistula.

"Plant the stuff and let's get out of this hole," Taken-Alive said.

She pulled the bag from her pocket.

"Vodka."

The gravel-colored pills seem to be getting heavier. She jammed the bag back in her pocket. "I don't belong here," she said, and started towards the door.

The downstairs door slammed shut and Cash's voice rose from the stairway. "Just as well we got rained out."

Bora whimpered something.

"Far as that goes, I ain't going to no Ohio, neither."

"You promised," she said.

Frantic, Hedy looked around for a closet. "Where can we hide?" she asked Taken-Alive. The footsteps were on the landing.

Cash, swinging the Coleman lamp, lurched into the room. His jaw dropped. "What the . . . ?" Bora, a few feet behind him, waved. His breath smelled sour with beer. "We were just leaving," Hedy said.

Cash flung out his arm. "Hold your horses. What do you think you're doing here?"

Hedy stiffened. "I should ask you that."

Bora slipped around them to the nightstand, took a candle from the drawer, and pulled a packet of matches from her jeans. The candledelight lit the photo of Bora, naked, surrounded by Canadian Mounties. "I was a blond then," she giggled.

Cash turned to Hedy and yelled, "Get on over to the house."

"Vodka."

"That's my bird," Bora said. She weaved as she bent to light her cigarette from the candle. "Vodka," she added.

Hedy motioned to mean the room and said to Cash, "Is this the bookcase you put together?"

He shuffled and looked at his feet and Taken-Alive adjusted his headband. Hedy started to walk past, when she heard snapping sounds and spun around just as corner of the waxed paper shot up in flames. Bora, on her knees, fumbled for the candle that had rolled

71

under the nightstand.

"Look what you gone and done," Cash yelled at Bora.

Taken-Alive grabbed the afghan and beat at the sparks. "Get up off the floor," he ordered Bora. Then he shouted over his shoulder, "Somebody find some water before this spreads."

Cash groped for the doorway. "I'm getting out."

Creamy smoke rose from the bedding. Shaking, Hedy steadied herself against the wall thinking somehow this burning room seemed familiar. Maybe she just remembered the blackened bricks of Szceczin Street where she had roller-skated as a kid.

"Give me your raincoat," Taken-Alive yelled. "It might still be damp."

Coughing, she wrapped the coat more tightly around her as she stumbled towards the hall.

"Vodka!"

Hedy turned, ran to the birdcage and jumped to reach the hook. Her skin felt seared. "Fire's gaining on us," she shouted.

Taken-Alive helped her swing down the cage. Vodka was an anthracite lump on the bottom. "Run," the Indian yelled.

"Mr. Alive!" Hedy shouted, pointing to Bora laying beside the bed. Taken-Alive dragged her away just as a section of plaster blistered, then crumbled to the floor.

"Carry her feet," Taken-Alive shouted to Cash.

"Is she dead?" Cash asked.

"Passed out," Taken-Alive panted.

Cash disappeared down the stairs. The birdcage bumped against Bora's toes as Hedy stooped to help Taken-Alive. Outside, sirens screamed. "Jump!" a voice boomed. Hedy held her breath and wiped her streaming eyes on her cuff. She ran to the window and stuck out her head. The incense bowl tumbled to the street.

Vince Gambino, chief of the Southeastern Number Five Company, yelled through a bull horn. "We got a net."

Choking between words, Hedy shouted, "It's only the bedroom. We'll be out the front door.

Hedy caught up with Taken-Alive dragging Bora across the landing. Walking backwards, he started down the stairs. Hedy gripped the birdcage. Timmy Sullivan, his arms around the nozzle of a throbbing firehose, ran up the steps two at a time. "Coming through," he yelled.

Another fireman in a yellow slicker held the hose a few feet behind Timmy. As they passed, Hedy flattened herself against the wall and Taken-Alive rolled Bora against the baseboard.

"Watch it!" Hedy screamed when a fireman stomped on her toe.

"Sorry, lady."

"Hey Charlie, here's the victims," a voice yelled. Two firemen swept Bora out the front door.

Hedy, limping behind Taken-Alive, paused on the stoop to catch her breath. Cash slouched on the curb across the street. Vince boomed through the bull horn, "Get away from the house." Hedy gripped the railing with one hand, the birdcage in the other and eased down the steps.

Three fire trucks, an ambulance, and a few squad cars were parked in the middle of the street. The rain had stopped and the slick cobblestones were rosy from the flares set out to block traffic. The double doors of the ambulance were opened. Two aides hovered over Bora.

"Stand back," Mario Russo shouted, using his billy club as a fence. Vodka, revived, flapped against the cage. Mr. Vecchio's terrier lunged and Hedy held the cage over her head as the dog, straining at the leash, danced under her arm.

"Down," Vecchio yelled. Mario grabbed the cage and swung it onto the front seat of the squad car.

Cash, Hedy, and Taken-Alive stood over Bora as an attendant with a coffee stain on his sleeve drew a pencil from his pocket. "You relations?" he asked Cash.

"Neighbors," he replied. "She don't have people around here."

The gold horse had slid across the chain and lay under Bora's ear. Her eyelids fluttered. "Was I hurt?" she mumbled. The aide blocked Hedy's hand as she reached to take Bora's pulse.

"I'm a nurse," Hedy snapped. "And if you ask me, she's more drunk than anything else."

"One of you got to come in the ambulance to check her into City Hospital," the attendant ordered.

Hedy pointed to Cash.

The aides wheeled the stretcher into the van. "Hop in," one yelled.

Cash nodded at Hedy and stepped aside. "You first."

She hesitated. Suddenly she realized that if she wanted to, she could spend the rest of her life walking ahead of Cash knitting. And he would be two steps behind unraveling.

"You're on your own," she whispered.

The jump seat beside the stretcher wobbled under Cash's weight.

A few people milled around the fire trucks while the men stowed the hoses. Hedy's foot throbbed. "Let's go home," she said to Taken-Alive.

"I put the bird on your back porch," Mario yelled.

Hedy stared at her house. Bora's soggy mattress lay across the curb. Pellets of rattan charcoal covered the steps. The stoop glittered with broken glass. Mr. Vecchio kicked a bottle into the street while the terrier lapped water from the incense bowl. Bora's bedroom windows were black holes—the eyes of a skeleton.

Hedy limped across the gutter and Taken-Alive offered his arm. She let go of his elbow at her doorway and walked ahead of him into the living room. He started to close the door.

"Leave it open," she said. A fresh breeze blew up from the bay.

"I'm coming back with a broom."

FIVE

Blue Haired Chickens

Tillie rolled back her sleeves. Just the thought of evicting Joe Vassky pepped her up. A month ago, she had sent that hippie a notice to get rid of his filthy chickens or to get out. He had three days left.

Tillie had put her farmhouse up for sale. The trailer next door that she rented to Vassky would be part of the deal. Pittsburgh and Wierton Industries had opened up the mines and was hiring again, and West Virginia real estate was booming. This was America, and maybe she, Tillie Kovalnus, an ordinary Lithuanian widow, could move into a split leveler in Shackle Heights. She had her eye on the ranchero model with a pool in the back yard. As she headed down the path from her driveway to the trailer she hummed, "The Duck Swims on the Tessina."

Next Wednesday, Vernon Hack, her prospective buyer, would be bringing his appraiser out for a thorough look at the premises before signing the contract so everything had to be shipshape. That meant no chickens.

At first she thought Vernon and his wife, Mervis, needed her house like they needed a washboard. Their glassy home in the Heights had a panoramic view of the barges sliding down the Shackle River towards Morgantown.

It turned out they wanted her place for their married kid. The rent from the trailer would pay the mortgage, and as Mervis put it, "We have to help Jamie." She had frowned, then added, "Within reason."

A dingy white chicken clucked at Tillie from the bannister around Vassky's stoop. With one hand on the small of her back to hold in the sciatica, she bent to pick up a chunk of red-dog gravel, but before she could toss it, the bird fluttered down into the pillow of ferns along the foundation. She pitched the pebble into the center of an inner tube smothered with cornflowers. The chicken was innocent. Vassky was the criminal.

She rolled her sleeves back another fold and banged on the door. "Who's knocking?" Vassky yelled from inside.

"Your landlady."

Yap, his orange hound, padded up to the screen.

Vassky, lean as a crowbar, unhooked the

door and said, "Hey, Mrs. Kovalnus, cup of tea?"

"I'm here to talk chickens."

He flipped his blond mane from his forehead and motioned her inside. The air in the living room smelled of Fels-Naptha. "I had a guy all set to buy them."

She pointed to the dingy chicken that was back on the railing. "Visitor?" She folded her arms across her chest. "I asked you to coop them up. They run around my yard like hooligans." She looked him straight in the eye. "They're not housebroken."

He propped his elbow on a shelf crammed with books. "You want me to put them in jail?"

Vassky's a Russian name, she thought. He might be a communist. There's no point in discussing reason with that kind of personality. "Where is this buyer?"

He adjusted the stake on a philodendron. "I don't want them killed. Pineapple said the guy lied about wanting them for eggs."

Everyone in Shackle knew her part-time man, Pineapple, had a brain the size of a barley pearl. Sciatica and all, she drew herself up to her full five feet. "When a person sells a chicken, it's all or nothing. Haul them off before Monday or the constable will."

All at once she smelled something burning. "My peach jelly," Vassky yelled. He ran into the kitchen, Tillie behind him.

Steam billowed over the stove. The top of the table was crowded with empty mustard and pickle jars and a block of paraffin weighed down a page of *Fanny Farmer*.

While he stirred and blew on the foam, she sneaked a look around. Swirls of buffed wax on the linoleum shone like brass hubcaps. Sprouts broke ground in peat-pots on the windowsill. She peered into the molten fruit. "You better skim," she said.

The sun fired the metal rims of his glasses. "I've never done that."

"Get me something to dump scum into."

He passed her a bowl that looked like a dog dish, then watched her slide the spoon over the foam and spill the pink bubbles into the bowl.

"You sure know your beans," he said.

"I haven't lived sixty-six years for nothing. Give me a ladle."

When she poured a curlicue of melted wax on top of the last jar, he grinned and asked, "Tea?"

"No thanks," she said, surprised that she wished she had more time to spend with Vassky. "Earls closes at noon and I got to get some poison for crickets."

"Toss the little fellows outside," he said. "What's the big deal?"

"I got important company coming."

Her station wagon was parked at the end of the drive. Thumbs hooked in his jeans, Vassky strolled beside her. Yap followed. A Rhode

Island Red was taking a dust bath in a rut and she stopped short. Yap, tongue dripping on her sneaker, stopped beside her. The bird looked up, hopped a few feet away, and started picking under its wing. "Lice," she snapped.

Vassky rolled a stone backwards and forwards with his toe, "I'll find a buyer."

She remembered the mangy rooster that crowed from her birdbath every morning, spoiling the last lap of her sleep. "Walk your talk," she said, opening the car door. The feet follow the heart, not the mouth, she thought.

Route Twenty-Two divided her land from the Shackle River. To distract herself from thoughts of chickens, she took a deep breath of musty air drifting up from the river bank. If this were the old country, I'd be picking mushrooms now instead of worrying about property, she thought. In Lithuania on Saturday mornings, everybody headed into the woods, the way in America they went to shopping malls.

Her favorite mushrooms sprouted between rocks. Brown, with silver ruffled edges like tambourines, their stalks grew this way and that. A bent one had a knobby head: a thinker. Another had a curved stem, the arm of a ballerina. She stifled a wave of homesickness and parked in front of the Southern States store.

Earl held up a bottle of chlordane. "This will kill anything," he beamed.

"I like their chirp." She wanted to make it clear that she was not that kind of person. "I'm only killing because important people are coming."

"And what would they think if they saw bugs?" he said, snapping open a paper bag.

By the time she got back to the car, the inside was as hot as a Bessemer furnace. The thought of monkeying with the sprayer made her feel even hotter. Then it occurred to her that Tuesday, when Pineapple came to hose the chicken litter from the bird bath and mow the lawn, he could also polish off the crickets—if she could talk him into it. He hated chemicals and claimed that fertilizer spilled on your skin caused warts.

She turned down the rutted lane leading to his shack. His front porch buckled under the weight of the refrigerator he kept beside the glider. "Handy in summer, cheaper to run in winter," he said.

She parked behind the coal pile. His pepper plants grew in an old kitchen sink resting on bricks. "Too high for rabbits and the drain's already there," he'd explained. Bill, the goat, was tethered to the door handle of a Chevy truck without wheels. She spotted Pineapple in his garden. "Mrs. Kovalnus," he called. Clumps of brown hair stood in spikes over his head. He had almost no shoulders, his neck simply sloped into his arms. He propped his shovel against a stack of tires and ambled towards her.

She shielded her eyes from the sun. "I got to man the election polls Tuesday so can you do me an extra favor?"

He reached down and twisted the blossom off a hollyhock. "Depends."

While she explained how to use the sprayer, he rolled flower petals into balls and flicked them at Bill's head. When she finished, he said, "Them poisons don't just kill what you set out to kill. They get ants, flies . . ."

"I'll add an hour to your check," she said.

"Gnats," he added. "And gnats fly in a ring so to call down the sun." He swooped his arm in a circle. "Ever see a hot day without gnats?"

She tried not to sound desperate. "Hack's bringing an appraiser."

Pineapple frowned. "Is he that Mister to the Missus with the blue hair?"

Usually Mervis' hair was covered with a net scarf. "It's gray, I think."

Pineapple spit over the hood of the truck. "Them ladies all put the same kind of stuff on it. Real hair don't come alike."

"You'll spray?"

He pulled a strip of turkish towel from his pocket and mopped his brow.

"I guess we got about enough sun."

She sighed with relief as she walked back to the car.

For some reason she took the mountain road home. At the top of the bluff, she slowed in front of the tall wooden post, stained to look weathered, with the name "Shackle Heights" written vertically. She turned on East Gardenia

Drive and pulled up in front of the ranchero. It was sided with upright khaki boards. A redwood deck circled the second floor. What a place to dry onions, she thought, then shot a glance down the street to make sure no one saw her idea. Suddenly, her polka-dot dress, her life, seemed out of place. Maybe there were two Americas, she thought, a level one to plant and a sideways one to climb. She cruised around the cul-de-sac, then started home.

The next morning the rooster sounded off at five. Sleep was impossible. While the coffee heated, she listed the things she had to do to whip the place into shape. First off, the garden had to look as if dental floss had been drawn between the rows.

It was slow going. By noon she was up to her neck in sweat. Sinister forces had marched on the squash blossoms.

"Use soapsuds on the vines," a voice behind her said.

She twisted around and looked up at Joe Vassky holding a Kroger bag. Embarrassed by her unprofessional appearance, she struggled to her feet.

He nodded at the bag. "Brought you something."

She waited for her sciatica to calm down, then picked up her trowel. The dishpan-size leaves moved. A rooster's head popped up and turned to the right, then to the left, a copper periscope. She waved the trowel and the head sunk below a broccoli leaf. "What can I say?" he mumbled.

"When will they be gone?"

"By tomorrow afternoon," he answered. She walked ahead of him and opened the kitchen door. He set the bag on the table and carefully lifted out a mottled egg. "These were tough to find. Most were under the chinaberry bush." He combed the hair from his eyes with his index finger.

She tried to put her question as delicately as she could. "You don't think because you brought me eggs that—?"

His gray eyes clouded. He reached into the bag again and brought out a jar of peach jelly. "I came to bring you this, then thought you'd get a kick out of fresh eggs, too."

She pretended to look at a tomato seed stuck on the counter top. "Coffee?" she asked quietly.

"I don't want to be a drag."

It took only a minute to get the pot simmering.

"I don't see any crickets," he said.

"They're under the baseboards in the living room," she said, handing him a mug.

His shirt flapped over his stomach as if it covered a cave, and she wished she had a pot of kugelis, a cake, poppyseed rolls. She opened the refrigerator and pulled out a crock of pickled mushrooms. "Like these?"

He peered into the brine. "They from the river bank?"

It took her a minute to catch on. "Krogers."

He made a circle with his fingers. "One day I caught them that big around in the meadow by the cottonwoods."

Caught, she thought. He was right. Mushrooms are not picked, but caught, their life short between suns. While she got him a plate and fork she wondered why it had never occurred to her to go mushroom picking in this country.

"I'll show you some of my best spots," he said, and added, "but everybody has to find his own place."

The next afternoon her tension over whether Vassky would get rid of the chickens was in full swing. On the way home after a long day of errands, her stomach wound tighter and tighter like a reel bringing in a fish. Then it snapped. It hit her that she didn't have to evict Vassky—or move for that matter. One voice inside her whispered stay put, another told her she was scared to move up, afraid of her own success. By the time she got to the driveway her mind had separated into the yolk of the farmhouse and the white of East Gardenia Drive. She slowed in front of the trailer. Usually, a flock of chickens clucked around the chinaberry bush; she checked the ditch for bantams. It was quiet as a funeral. Vassky, his back towards her, was cultivating his corn. She was glad she didn't have to face him.

The next morning, election day, she slept through the twittering of the sparrows. Late for the polls, she waved as she shot past Pineapple in his truck on Route Twenty-Two. The primary was held in the elementary school. Checking the voter list and putting up with Janet Thackery's busybody cracks was hot, thankless work. Around three, just when she slumped back with a coke, Mervis and Vernon Hack stepped into the auditorium. A tiny man wearing fishbowl glasses trotted behind Vern. Tillie's nose for trouble told her this was the appraiser. Mervis' toy poodle, Fifi, quivered in her arms. The creases in her white slacks were sewn in as straight as if her legs were staked. "I called your house and a Mr. Pineapple said you'd be here," she said.

Vern nodded to the man at his elbow. "This here's Mac McGinnis, come down from Union-town." Mac held out his squirrel paw hand. "We had a closing today but the buyer couldn't get his loan." Vern jabbed Mac in the ribs. "No dough, no go, right?"

Mervis' voice sounded greased by her violet lipstick. "So we thought we'd come out to your place now instead of tomorrow."

Tillie froze. Even with the chickens gone and Pineapple's cleanup, she wanted to check the place first. "I can't leave the polls."

"Oh, go on," Janet piped up.

Tillie's mind groped for an excuse, but Vernon took her arm. Reluctantly, Tillie followed Mervis from the auditorium.

Stuck behind a red light, she lost sight of Vern's Cadillac. Pineapple might be right, she thought looking at the sky. The first stormy day in weeks; he must have killed some gnats. When she drove past her garden, she wondered why the scatter rugs hung over the fence. "I smell hot water," she whispered. Pineapple's truck was parked on the lawn, tailgate hanging down like a panting tongue. Vern was pacing around the lily bed. "Let's get in before the rain," he shouted above the wind. Mervis, with Fifi under her arm, struggled out of the back seat. Tillie looked around for Pineapple. But whatever he was up to, there was no turning back. She led the Hacks and McGinnis across the porch and pushed open the screen.

A brown hen flapped around her ankles. Tillie lifted her head. All twenty of Vassky's chickens fluttered, squawked, and strutted around the living room. Pineapple stood in the center, his arms out in front of him wiggling his fingers and shouting, "Don't stir them up."

"What the—" Vern said. Mervis screamed.

Vern spun around and snapped, "Don't start that."

Fifi, her bulging eyes on the rooster, bolted from Mervis' arms. She screamed again and lunged after the dog.

"They was all right up until a minute ago,"

Pineapple yelled, grabbing a bird's leg. "See what you gone and done?" The window blind clacked against the pane and Tillie swerved past a Rhode Islander on her way to close the sash.

Pineapple must have seen her face. "Crickets all gone," he yelled.

Mervis, chasing Fifi, ran between them.

"Vassky paid me to keep them until he could sell. Free food for them, crickets all gone for you. Only I thought you was to be gone all day." He grabbed a bird off the arm of a chair.

McGinnis stood beside Tillie with a pad and pencil. "The floors will need resanding. I'm going to write that down." The black hen pecked at his toe and he jerked his foot away.

Pineapple stroked the bird's neck. "Chicken lime's the best thing in the world for hardwood."

Fifi stood on her hind legs to sniff at a hen on the coffee table. As Mervis scooped up the dog, the net scarf slipped off her head. Sure enough, her hair was cornflower blue. Tillie squinted at her through the down-filled air, and without knowing why started to laugh.

"Perhaps we could come at a more convenient time," McGinnis said.

"If I didn't want the property so bad I'd never come back," Vern snapped.

A black feather drifted between Tillie's face and Vern's. She puffed up her cheeks, pursed her lips and blew. Vern jumped backwards and grabbed the back of a chair to steady himself, then yelled, "Get on out to the car, Mervis." He walked out the door, McGinnis at his heels.

A few minutes after the Hacks left, the chickens quieted.

Pineapple toyed with his belt, a frayed clothesline.

"Told you not to stir them up."

Marshmallows of chicken litter stuck to the coffee table, the desk, the chairs. A feather swung from the bottom of a lampshade. A rooster, pecking at lint, milled around the sofa.

"Mr. Hack sure was ready to buy," Pineapple said. "Before you blew him away."

Tillie walked over and picked up a hen. It flapped, then settled in the crook of her arm. "Soon as I catch my breath, let's get these birds back to Vassky."

"But he told me—."

She smiled at the chicken's head. "Everybody finds his own place."

SIX

Sweet Chickadee of Grace

I'm a Michaeletki Sister, not a prophet. How could I know if Zacko would lose his mind? Some said he was already crazy. But to me it seemed his heart had turned to salt, that's all, just drawing all the sorrow of the world inside.

The tenth graders had gone home for the day. Zacko stood beside me in front of the bird feeder bracketed to the wall outside the classroom window. The redwood tray was wrist high in sunflower seed hulls. "You're not hearing me," I said.

A drop of sweat rolled down his thin neck and into his frayed collar. "Wrong, Sister Veronica." His eyes glittered behind his aviator glasses, tinted light brown. "I hear everything." He looked out the window. "Clouds rubbing up against each other." He nodded to the bulb garden on the sill. "Roots squeaking through them

91

stones." A chickadee hopped to the edge of the feeder, then soared to a nearby jack pine. "Wings."

Zacko had slipped back inside his own world, a strange one, for sure. But aren't most inner worlds? Take my roommate, Sister Felicity. The compartments of her brain, if there are such things, must look like cells of a hive, which was why only another drone could understand her: I couldn't. And the inside of Father Casimer's head must seethe like a jungle. He said the prince of darkness was fishing for his soul. I pictured a bright red devil hovering over a swamp deep in Father's chest, pitchfork poised, ready to spear Father's slippery old soul as it swam past.

I reached for the empty seed cup and a dropping stuck to my white sleeve. "Tonight's the night I'm going to your house to speak to your dad," I said, trying to sound as if it were an everyday event.

"So who lives in a house?" Zacko asked bitterly.

I knew he and his father, Pete, lived in a trailer. Born in Shackle, a mining town same as any other in West Virginia, I had gone to high school with Zacko's mother. She left Pete about a year ago. My landlady had asked why a middle-aged lady like Clara Gabonas would run off with an electrician from Pittsburgh. The answer was in my bones, not my head. The mines had all but shut down, and Shackle fed on grit and commodity cheese. Clara, a cashier at K mart, had been laid off. Pete was dying of black lung, and Zacko, their only kid, was sinking down a shaft of dark rage.

"Don't mind your home," I said softly. Zacko ran his hand through his hair, a collie's winter coat. I bent to lift the the ten pound sack of "Sing Along." His arm brushed my shoulder as he grabbed the bag.

Suddenly a shrill voice yelled, "Hey, Whacko-Zacko, I need a buck for cigarettes." Sally McAllister leaned against the doorway. Her eye caught mine and she held up her gym suit. "Forgot this." Wire earrings swung to her shoulders; her pink shirt needed to be ironed, as did her pleated slacks. From across the room I could see the shine of green eye shadow. "Come on with me to the Dairy-Deli," she coaxed Zacko, who looked around the walls as if trying to find another door.

"See you later, Sister," he mumbled, and I turned to lower the blinds.

Sally's voice echoed in the hall. "Wait for me, Zacko."

The corridors of Saint Stanislaus High smelled of black bananas and kerosene. The night lights turned the blistered paint on the walls into a topography map. When the mines were booming, the Church had poured money into Shackle. Now the parish wormed out contributions from the miners who had been cut back to two shifts a week. Sometimes at Mass, my jaw tightened when I saw the bulging envelopes printed with family names, Gabonas, Spassky, Nicolouskas, Bronchek, piled in the collection basket. There was nothing wrong with the poor buying hope, I thought. Another voice inside me asked, but is it wrong to sell it? I checked that the school door locked behind me.

My apartment was a block away. I remembered Felicity had asked Father Casimer, our parish priest, for supper and I stepped up my pace. Felicity and I shared the attic of Miss Morrison's tumble-down Victorian house. Built as a mansion, it was later a rooming house for railroad men. Then when the B&O folded, the upper stories were chopped up into apartments. As I hurried into the hallway, Miss Morrison's whine sailed from her wainscoted office, once a drawing room. "This chill eats my every bone."

I waved at the shriveled gray head, barely visible above the top of the partners desk, osteoporosis having quartered her height. "Is Father here yet?" I asked.

"He brought you and Sister a Whitman's Sampler."

I sighed and climbed the winding staircase.

During dinner, my mind strayed from the chitchat about the Pittsburgh Pirates. Felicity smiled at me, her curly blond bangs softening the starched cuff of her veil. "Are we brooding?"

Like most kindergarten teachers, Felicity had trouble speaking adult after hours. "I have an appointment with a parent tonight," I said.

Father lifted the top crust of his pie to check the filling. Felicity's blueberries glistened with cornstarch.

"Pete Gabonas," I added.

Father lowered the crust. He disapproved of what he called "fraternization with the community." He looked at me as if expecting justification.

I swallowed a mouthful of dough. "I think Zacko's hallucinating."

"Do you think? Or do you know?" Father asked. He slid the plate of uneaten pie against his wine glass.

I shrugged and raised my palms.

The overhead light caught the whites of his eyes. "You are ambivalent," he said, holding up his index finger. "And ambivalence is the germ of evil that infects the goodness of right and the malice of wrong until each sickens and dies."

Felicity stood and picked up my dish. "Maybe Zacko smokes grass with the kids behind the ball field."

Father winced.

"Maybe he's mentally ill," I said. I struggled for words to defend my intuition, then gave up and decided to keep it simple. "He needs a psychiatrist. There's a clinic in Morgantown."

"Catholic?" Father asked.

I choked on a sip of water. When I was twenty, I had taken vows. That was fifteen years ago. For the past five I had become more and more impatient with the parochial vision of the older religious. Instead of a rock, their house seemed built on shifty-eyed bickering. "I'm more worried about Zacko than dogma," I said.

Father's knuckles whitened around the stem of his glass. His shoulders moved forward, a grackle hunching up to fly. "Then get down on your knees," he said.

I dug my spoon handle into the warp of the placemat. He leaned closer and hissed, "Beg Saint Michael the Archangel to protect your Zacko from the prince of darkness who roams through the world fishing for men's souls."

Back to the swamp, I thought. Prayer—Father's reaction to every problem. As if action would require penance. He drew back. A minute later, he and Felicity picked up their baseball talk. Bored, I excused myself as soon as I could, buttoning my cape on the way out the door. There was an hour to kill before meeting Pete.

Along the sidewalk a few marigolds had survived the November frost. Spindly privet spears had shot up during yesterday's thaw. The bell tower of Saint Stanislaus loomed over the slate roof. Inside, the church was dark and fragrant with burning wax and chrysanthemums bundled on each side of the altar. I knelt before the tier of flickering candles at the feet of the Holy Family and prayed for humility, then to be forgiven for the vanity of thinking I deserved it.

When I left the church, on the spur of the moment I decided to go to the cemetery on the other side of the wall. Frequently I stopped at the Zedonas plot. I stooped and dragged the spray of soggy lilies off my mother's stone, then crossed myself and bowed my head. Something rustled behind a crypt. I shrugged and bowed my head again, but looked up at the sound of a cough and the scrape of a match. Someone tall rounded the corner of the mausoleum. A red tip of a cigarette swung at his side. Before I had time to be afraid I thought I recognized Zacko's beige jacket. Since my cape was dark as my veil, I was probably impossible to spot. He stood beside a cypress tree and raised his arm. For a second the cigarette glow reflected on the brown-tinted glasses, then he crossed the Kovalesky's plot and stopped beside a life-sized statue of a kneeling angel. Moonlight polished the silvery head. Slowly, Zacko leaned and ran his hand over the stone hair, the peak of the folded wing. His fingers moved on down the throat, then quickly slid and cupped the breast. I stepped back into the shadows and stared at the dead lilies at my feet. When I lifted my head he was gone.

The skin on my chest tingled. I pulled my cape tight, then hurried to the cemetery gate, then looked up and down the street. Under the light, a man in a beige canvas jacket unlocked the door of a pickup. He flipped his cigarette butt into the gutter, then hopped into the front seat. He was taller than he seemed in the cemetery. How stupid that I thought this man was Zacko.

A few blocks down the road where Pete

lived, the streetlights ended and the pavement turned into a red-dog gravel path. The walls and turrets of the Monongahela Penitentiary loomed over one side of the road and asbestos-shingle shacks lined the other. Cabbage gardens dotted the hillside like chenille spreads. Gabonas' trailer rusted along the muddy track that led down to the Shackle River. The porch light glowed. When I rapped, an old beagle, asleep in a child's empty swimming pool, lifted its head.

Pete opened the door.

I smiled and said, "It's been a long time, Pete." He motioned me inside, and in one step I was beside the sofa. A kerosene pot-burner took up most of the living room. Flames snapped behind its glass door that was black with soot.

A dot of blood dried on Pete's chin, and his damp cowlick bristled. "What can I get you, Sister? Coffee?" He held up his thumb and fore-finger, "Little nip?"

Shackle hospitality: a house hot enough to roast a chicken in, and whiskey.

"Nothing," I said.

Pete dragged a chrome chair from the kitchen and sat opposite me, apparently not wanting to share the couch. He fumbled at his breast pocket. "You don't mind if I have a smoke." Without waiting for an answer, he turned and ran a match down a rough slit between the paneling. "Zacko's over to the Dairy-Deli."

I sat on the edge of the cushion. "You must

have noticed his. . . ." I glanced at the snapshot of Clara propped on the television set. "Distance," I said.

"Teenagers," he said impatiently. He inhaled, then doubled over, one rasping breath and cough followed by another, the sound of wheels turned by oxen to bring up water from ancient river beds. He lifted his head and wiped his mouth on the back of his wrist.

"Why are you bent on killing yourself?" I asked.

He studied the ash of his cigarette. "You should know."

I didn't know. And I also wouldn't press to hear more problems than I could solve. "I'll get to the point," I said. Pete studied his knuckles. "Zacko needs a psychiatrist."

Pete's hand tightened into a fist. "You think he's crazy?"

"I think he is living inside his mind," I said before I realized my answer made no sense.

Pete walked into the kitchen and spoke over the stove built into the room divider. "His mother took crazy." Pete rubbed the back of his neck. "You think them quacks can cure a nut?" He pointed to his chest. "Besides, I ain't paying to fix what she broke."

I struggled to keep my voice calm. "There's a free clinic in Morgantown. Do I have your permission to refer him?"

Pete's eyes widened. "No one asked me if I wanted the kid in the first place."

My face flushed with annoyance as well as the heat. I stood. "God expects us to nurture our children."

Pete jumped in front of me to open the door. "Don't get me wrong." He motioned to the stove burners crusted with grease. "I try to feed him good."

I stared at Pete until his shoulders slumped and his eyes dropped. "Send him, send him," Pete said. "What's the difference?"

I stepped off the porch into the weeds. "God Bless you," I called as he closed the door.

It was noon the next day before I managed to get to the telephone in the teacher's lounge. The clinic could give Zacko an appointment tomorrow. I hung up and made a mental note to arrange for Mr. Harvey, the janitor, to drive Zacko to Morgantown.

Felicity stood in the doorway of the lounge. "Do you have Sally McAllister?" she asked, crossing to the juice machine. I nodded. "I hate to see them grow up too soon," she added.

I pictured Sally's denim skirt straining against her thighs. "When her mother's drunk she saddles Sally with the six younger kids," I said. "Her father, he's a prison guard, makes her fix his supper at five in the morning when he comes home from the graveyard shift." The bell rang and I followed Felicity into the hall.

At the end of the day during homeroom prayer, Zacko stared out the window. Father's blessing droned to a stop over the intercom, and I dismissed the class. Zacko passed my desk and I asked him to wait. He paused, an island in the river of kids scrambling to the ball field. I opened my desk drawer and pulled out a plastic bag bulging with chunks of fat tinged with red beef. "Do you want to hang the suet?" I asked.

Zacko turned to the window. "Snow," he said.

The white tracer-bullets pounded the glass. Zacko didn't look at the bag I handed him, but walked to the window, pushed it open, and leaning outside, hung the fat on its hook. "The appointment is tomorrow." I said. "You can meet Mr. Harvey on the front steps around noon. It's his day to go to Morgantown."

Zacko stared down at me, wound off his glasses and shoved them in his breast pocket. His blue eyes darted around the room as if it were a cage. He turned and said, "You can't make me," then strode out the door.

My head throbbed and my throat felt rough. I sneezed and figured I must be catching cold, probably from Pete's overheated trailer. Halfway across the ball field it occurred to me to make sure Mr. Harvey would take Zacko. And I had better clear it with Father. Although the teaching nuns didn't report to him, he was in charge of facilities. Ahead of me the church spire, glistening with sleet, skewered the mist.

I found Father on the rectory porch tossing rock salt on the cement. He yelled above the wind. "This weather's going to get worse before it gets better."

I told him about Zacko's appointment.

Father scowled and rolled up the empty salt bag. "I'm going uptown to get more of this. Tell Mr. Harvey I said it was all right. I think he's waxing the back hall in the school."

My body bent into the wind as I walked. I reached in my pocket and pulled out a tissue. Mr. Harvey's pickup was not in front of the cellar entrance where it was usually parked. I banged on the door, then discovered, although it was after five, the door was unlocked. It clanged shut behind me. "Mr. Harvey," I called. I stuck my head into the janitor's workroom. A gust of wind rattled the pane. I stepped back into the hall. The building was chilly from the night thermostat setting. The corridors were black tunnels but for squares of light shining through the transoms of the closed classroom doors. The auditorium was empty, only an amber glow shone beneath the door of the gym. I pushed down on the bar of the lock and winced at the smell of sneakers. Suddenly Sally's voice sobbed, "No. Don't."

Zacko and Sally struggled on a stack of exercise mats. Her skirt was rolled around her waist. Her fist, twined in his hair, was pulling back his head. He writhed on top of her and she strained to rise from under his weight. Shreds of matting, like burst milkweed pods, tumbled in the air. "Let me go," she screamed.

Stunned, I turned and ran, not knowing or caring where. Nothing. I had seen nothing, I told myself dashing into the girl's bathroom, the first sanctuary I found. I stood in the entrance, and tried to catch my breath, the force of the spinning world pinning my back to the door. A ray of light filtered through the pebbled glass window and shone on my skirt. It took a few minutes before I could make out the fixtures. Knees quivering, I stood over a sink. "Mary-Lou" was scrawled in pink lipstick across the paper towel holder. The tap whined as I splashed cold water on my eyes. My breathing calmed; I dried my face. Why was I so bent out of shape? I wondered. Zacko and Sally were necking in the gym, that's all, and I best go back and send them home and stop hiding in the bathroom like a criminal.

I hurried to the gym and called, "Anybody there?"

Zacko and Sally were gone. Not even an indentation scarred the mat; only a tuft of padding trailed from a tear in the corner. Relief, then the shame of my cowardice hit me. I lowered my eyes and walked away.

"Working late, Sister?" Mr. Harvey called from the doorway of the boys' shower room. It took me a second to remember why I was looking for him.

"Zacko Gabonas needs a ride to—"

"Morgantown," Mr. Harvey said. "I ran into Father uptown."

Around midnight that night, I lay in bed and stared out the window at the curve of Mount Sorry-Dog. The snow had tapered off and the moon flashed behind foamy clouds. Years ago, white pine had forested the mountain. But after the strip mines pulled out, wispy jack pines, secondary growth, had sprouted up like everlasting dandelions. I thought of Sally, then buried my head in the pillow.

Midmorning the next day I spotted Zacko walking out the door beside Mr. Harvey. My heart was relieved that he would be getting help, but my stomach still churned—from the virus no doubt. By lunchtime I felt too sick to eat anything except peanut butter and cheese crackers from the machine in the lounge. "Isn't it awful?" Felicity said, biting open a bag of potato chips.

I held up a cracker. "Cardboard."

She raised her eyebrows. "I thought Zacko would be the only thing on your mind." I frowned. "You mean you don't know Zacko raped Sally?" Felicity set her tomato juice on the table and pulled out a chair. "At least that's what she says."

It took me a minute to grasp what Felicity had said. Then my stomach clenched. "Why did she tell you that?" I asked.

Felicity sat down. "She didn't. Casper told me."

Casper Harrington was Sally's homeroom teacher. A lay instructor, he taught American

Goverment. I took a deep breath, ready to tell Felicity about the scene in the gym. Then it occurred to me if I spoke up I could become another nail in Zacko's coffin.

"Who would have believed it?" Felicity asked.

"I don't," I said. I carefully folded the cellophane wrapper into a tiny square keeping my head lowered so Felicity couldn't see behind my eyes. Suddenly I remembered the months my boyfriend and I had made love in the back seat of his father's station wagon while I struggled to accept the will of my calling. During that time, I chatted with my parents over ordinary suppers.

"You're not paying attention," Felicity said. She stood and picked up the can. "Mrs. McAllister said she'd never rest until Zacko's behind bars."

I pressed my finger on the wrapper to hold down the folds. "Do the police know?"

Felicity tossed the can into the trash. "Ask Casper."

I found him eating lunch on the stage in the auditorium. *The Wall Street Journal* lay beside his paper plate. I unfolded a metal chair and sat beside him and asked, "Are the police after Zacko?"

Casper lowered his sandwich, "Apparently, Sally came home last night acting funny. Mrs. McAllister finally dragged out a story about Zacko raping the kid. Red McAllister went crazy and dragged Sally down to the station. He was really pissed when they questioned Zacko, then let him go." Casper dropped a crust and brushed off his fingers. "The McAllisters never gave a damn about the kid until they had a chance to show off how self-righteous they are."

I cleared my throat to drive the anger from my voice. "Zacko's strange, but gentle enough. Besides, he and Sally are friends," I said.

"The law doesn't allow for that," he said stiffly. "Rape is the act without consent of the victim. All Sally has to prove is that she said 'no' and Zacko is a dead duck. Shame there wasn't a witness."

"Why didn't they book him?" I asked quickly.

Casper rose and folded his chair. "Cops don't believe girls like Sally. You know Captain Kowalscz? I'll bet he laughed for an hour after the McAllisters left the station."

For the rest of the afternoon, I seethed over the injustice being done to Zacko, telling myself Sally's "no" was teasing. If Zacko were found guilty and sentenced, the inmates and guards (I pictured Red McAllister's florid cheeks) would torment the life out of him and surely he would crack. I pictured the Shackle River that circled the Penitentiary like a dead worm.

Home, I paused in the hall to flip through my mail. My stomach had calmed but my head pounded. All I could think of was a cup of whisky tea. "Tired Sister?" Miss Morrison called.

"A touch of flu," I said passing her doorway.

As I mounted the bottom step she called, "Anything happen to that McAllister girl after she lied to the police?"

I gripped the bannister. "What should happen?"

"She ought to be locked up."

"Why?" I asked, annoyed.

"I see the tramp around town."

I paused on the stairs. "What if she's innocent?" I asked.

"Those kind never are," she said smugly.

Upstairs, I made a cup of tea laced with bourbon. I considered the bottle for a minute, then added another drop and stirred it with the tip of my finger while I stared out the window. Old Sorry-Dog, drooping his tail of trees on one end and bony low bluff on the other, seemed more down and out than ever. I sat on the bed. Was there anything I could do for Zacko? A second later I was prowling the room. Saint Teresa's "Way of Perfection" lay on the dresser. My eyes closed as I quickly turned to a text, an old game I played with myself, believing that whatever passage I first saw was a special message. I opened my eyes and the words floated right up from the page and quivered in the air. I read and re-read the sentence — her warning not to cheat the truth for the cause of blind love.

I eased off my oxfords and bent to shove them beside the bed. One of the laces had snapped while I was coaching the soccer team and I had tied the frayed string together in three places. How long ago, a month? A sunflower seed was stuck in the raggedy knot. My cheeks felt warm. I tossed the shoes in the closet and pulled out my Sunday pair, all the while remembering the Mother General checking for mud on our heels, for stains on our collars. Somewhere in my life the discipline of the convent had slipped.

I pulled a nightgown from the drawer. Or maybe it was me who was slipping. Letting myself go. Thinking mean thoughts about Felicity and Father, and worst, trying to make judgments about Zacko's guilt or innocence, clearly outside my province. Report what I had seen to the police, then forget it, I told myself

I dropped the flannel nightgown over my head. Now I sounded exactly like the older clerics, the puppets. Where was all that free will God gave me? Free will to keep my mouth shut, to shield Zacko? Or a fancy rationale for someone who hasn't the stomach to turn the kid in.

I can't give in to my weak moral fiber, I thought. Tomorrow, I best call Captain Kowalscz. All I could do for Zacko would be to pray he would have the strength to accept whatever happened. I finished my tea and went to bed, comforted by the warm quilt of righteousness.

At dawn my head was clear. I dressed and braved the howling storm. In my classroom, Mr.

Harvey's morning blast of heat banged through the radiators. Kids shrieked on the playground. The bell rang and I stood to go to assembly.

As I passed the library, Sally stepped in front of me. I followed her up the steps to the auditorium. The back of her ankle was rubbed raw from the strap on her pumps, a runner slanting across her polka-dot stockings. Plastic earrings dangled like ornaments on a Christmas tree flung in the trash.

Instead of turning into the auditorium, I slipped into the lounge and sat on the edge of the end table, then dialed the Shackle police station. I asked to speak to the Captain. My speech was rehearsed. If he offered to come by after school to take my statement, I would insist upon going to the station. Miss Morrison would never survive the scandal of a squad car in front of her house.

The kids were singing "Winged Grace Guide my Soul."

I held the phone for a few minutes before Kowalscz's gruff voice answered, "Yes?"

I dropped the receiver onto the telephone. Free will or no free will, I had to wait until my knees stopped shaking before I could stand.

I turned to the entrance to the hall, then stopped. Over the doorway, the sallow sun touched the Crucifix and turned the alloy patina to gold. I crossed myself and whispered, "Go down, prince of that dark world."

SEVEN

Binkas Sausage

Stella Binkas dangled a loop from her fist and said, "I grind it by hand."

"Do you add preservatives?" the customer asked.

Stella coiled the sausage onto white butcher paper and dropped it on the scale. "Perfectly normal," she replied.

"Then make it two pounds."

While Stella rang up the last sale of the day, her sister, Jenny, finished the Fourth of July window display of sausage tins: round cookie cans with George Washington's face painted on each lid, and a balloon captioned "Bite a Binkas" billowing from his lips. Another one of Stella's half-assed ideas, Jenny thought. She cracked her chewing gum and checked the calendar over the register. This time next week she would be on her first vacation—provided her sister didn't wheedle her out of it.

Stella's rutabaga face rose from behind the counter. "Sissy, please don't go to no Grand Canyon."

Jenny's lips tightened. Every year Stella manipulated Jenny into socking her vacation money back into the Binkas family business. Last summer she gave up two grand for the cyclone fence. This year Stella was hinting about a blinking neon sign. Jenny balanced the last tin on the pile, stepped back, and said over her shoulder, "I'm thirty-five years old—"

"Thirty-eight," Stella said.

"And I never been but ten miles from Conkling Street. For the last time I'm going, I'm going."

Stella snapped out the light, then shuffled across the planked floor like a bear. Her flowered housedress was covered by a white bibbed apron. Ashes crumbled from the cigarette between her lips. "Remind me tomorrow to order more sodium nitrite from the wholesaler." She reached for a box in the rack holding crackers. "I got Louie's Choco-Chips."

Jenny glanced at Stella and said, to lighten the mood, "I did the books and we come out with, like, twelve percent profit."

"Chicken seed," Stella said. "Just wait until the remodelment."

Maybe no Binkas was ever satisfied. Forty years ago, Jenny's parents, Stella, and Pa's sister, Gryta, left Lithuania and came to Baltimore.

Jenny was born when Stella was fifteen. A few years later Ma, a big-boned woman with a booming voice (Stella was a dead ringer for her) died of heart failure and Pa buried himself in the business. He and Stella would sit at the kitchen table talking showrooms, a chain of outlets coast to coast, franchises, the day when Binkas would be a household word on the lips of America. Then five years ago Pa died from a heart attack in the apartment above the one-room store.

Stella pulled the blind down over the front window. "In the new sausage mart no more roll shades, either. Jalousies only."

Jenny adjusted the thermostat on the freezer. "Want to bet Louie's home and waiting for supper?"

"That boarder might be more trouble than he's worth," Stella said, standing on tiptoe to lock the grill over the door.

Jenny followed Stella onto the wooden back porch that swayed under her weight, then walked across the yard. A fresh pile of broken bottles glittered in the summer twilight. The cyclone fence hadn't kept the kids out. They hopped over the roofs like squirrels and tossed down tin cans, rubber balls and hubcaps as fast as Jenny raked. She mounted the steps to the row-house next door. Stella bought it from Doc Wallinski, the dentist, when he retired, the idea being the sisters would live in it while remodeling the first floor as an addition to the store. As soon as the connecting wall between the houses came down, Stella and Jenny planned to move to a rancher in the suburbs, buy a riding mower, a barbeque pit, and commute to work like everybody else.

From Wallinski's porch, the Patapsco River shone like a mirror. Ships' derricks peaked like grasshopper legs over the harbor. Diesel fumes drifted up from Laske's chandlers on Aliceanna Street. A tugboat dragged a freighter into the shipping channel and Jenny caught a glimpse of a figure leaning over the rail. A Greek flag fluttered from the stern, and suddenly her throat tightened with longing to be on that deck.

Stella handed her the Choco-Chips. "Hold these, please." She pulled up the porch window. The new meat locker had been installed where the back door used to be. The front door had been replaced by a floor-to-ceiling showroom window.

Stella sat sidesaddle on the sill and swung her legs over the ledge and into the kitchen. Then Jenny perched on the window frame. A splinter pricked her leg. "Is it asking too much to live in a house with a goddamn door?" she asked, flexing her slim calf and watching her stocking split into a tiny ladder down to her ankle.

Stella glanced at the runner. "Next pair, get with hearts sewn on."

Jenny slammed down the screen.

"Like Our Lady of Fatima would wear," Aunt Gryta called, "if she could afford them."

Gryta wore tennis shoes and a long black taffeta dress with an amber broach at the neck. Stella kissed her cheek, then straightened the bobby pin that held a paper tulip in the old woman's hair. Gryta cut the Sunday comics into paper flowers to hold her snowy cowlick. Today was Flash Gordon day. "Did you come directly home from Mass?" Stella asked.

Gryta's watery blue eyes focused on the cookies. "Chocos," she yelled.

Jenny balanced the box on top of her head. "They're Louie's."

Stella shouted above the hiss of tap water. "He won't miss one."

"You know he carps about every lousy dime," Jenny said. Gryta's eyes reddened. Jenny tipped her head and caught the box as it dropped. "What the hell." She tore back the lid. When Gryta reached in, a ticket stub dropped from her pocket. "Did you play the lotto again?" Jenny asked.

Stella, cradling an enamel pot, kicked the refrigerator door shut. "You promised to stop." she said.

Gryta studied the stub on the floor. "The minute the Eucharist passed my lips, God mentioned a number." When no one was home, Gryta prowled the rooms and pocketed loose change. She said she only played the numbers under strict instructions from the Blessed Mother.

The window rattled open and Louie's

115

embossed boot rounded the sill. "What a day."
He ducked his fuzzy gray head under the frame.
"The damn Metro bus conked out on Eastern
Avenue."

"They fix it?" Stella asked.

"Packed us on the number twenty-one if
that's what you call fixing," Louie grumbled.

Jenny fluffed up her blond bangs that sometimes got stringy at the end of a hot day.

Louie scowled at the torn box top. "I don't
pay for no empties." His features were bird
sharp in his pointy face; his round eyes flat as
overcoat buttons.

"Gryta only took but one," Jenny said.

"All or nothing."

"Pay half," Stella ordered.

Louie munched a Choco while he dropped
seventy cents on the table, one coin at a time.

Upstairs in her bedroom, Jenny pulled on
jeans, then studied the photo of a cowboy riding
a pinto on the brochure tucked into the corner
of the mirror. His tight black shirt was open to
his waist as he leaned on the pommel and gazed
into the Grand Canyon. She opened the drawer
and took out the packet of guided tour leaflets
and the money she had withdrawn yesterday.
Saturday she would be off to desert suns, moons,
nightclubs—anything could happen.

She gathered her towel and washcloth and
slipped down the hall. While she dried her face
in the bathroom she stared at Louie's thin gray
T-shirt draped over the shower rod. He had been

boarding with them a month. A friend of a friend referred him to Stella, saying Louie needed a place to stay until he got on his feet. His wife had taken the kids to her mother's in Steubenville. Jenny peered at his tiger-striped shorts piled on the floor. Men were a mystery, she decided. No matter where she pretended to look she was looking at the line down the front of them. She wondered if they cared about anything else.

Louie banged on the door. "Stella says come eat."

Gryta, her eyes squeezed shut, prayed over a platter of cabbage. "And furthermore," she droned, "everybody should have everything they want. Within reason. World leaders must . . ."

Jenny pictured herself on a donkey riding down the Canyon. "Psst." Louie hissed, and pointed to her dish. She shook her head. He leaned with his fork poised over a boiled potato. Without looking up, Stella capped the potato with the bowl of a serving spoon.

"Children, too . . ." Gryta mumbled. Stella touched the old woman's arm. "World peace. Amen."

Louie turned to Jenny. "When do you leave for the wild west?"

"Don't remind me," Stella said.

"Why not?" Jenny snapped.

"In the first place, people who go down that canyon never come back."

"Then everyone would be piled up on the

117

bottom and it wouldn't be a canyon," Jenny said.

"Smart ass," Stella said.

"Bought your ticket?" Louie asked.

"I got the cash upstairs. The ticket's being held at the station."

Louie wiped his plate with a rye crust. "Why spend money when you could knock around Bal'more for free?"

"You ever travel?" she asked.

Louie leaned back and rubbed his stomach. "Someday I'll show you my slides of Akron."

"I want to go where the colors make a difference," she said softly.

"Talking colors," Stella said. "You think the word 'Binkas' should be in red or green neon?"

Jenny slammed down her fork.

"What did I say?" Stella asked.

Jenny stood and lifted her empty plate. "Binkas, Binkas, Binkas."

Stella's voice was gruff. "Leave the dishes for me to catch after the movie show."

"We're going to watch the Pellagrini's VCR," Gryta said. "They rented Rapers of the Sun."

Louie winked at Jenny. "Want to talk about canyons?" She picked up her beer and followed him into the living room where he snapped on "The Dating Game."

Stella had bought Doc Wallinski's waiting-room furniture. Jenny sat on the vinyl sofa opposite the plate glass window of the new

Binkas showroom. Two women on the street stared into the room as they strolled past. Jenny tucked in her shirttail.

"Why's Stella so bent out of shape about you taking a week off?" Louie asked.

Jenny rolled her chewing gum wrapper into a ball. "The more I kick into Binkas, the faster we'll have the new store. Pa wanted a big showroom."

"No offense, but he's dead, right?"

"It's a big deal to Stel, too." Jenny took the gum from her mouth while she sipped beer.

"He must have drummed that shit into her head."

Jenny put the gum back in her mouth. "Maybe, maybe not. I think people get born with ideas they inherit." She tapped her chest. "Think how I'm crazy to travel."

Louie turned down the TV sound. "Why don't you drive out?" he asked.

"I can't drive."

He stared at the indoor-outdoor carpet. "Buses suck. I want to get me that '79 Duster Steve Spassky has for sale in his front yard."

"Go for it."

Louie put his hand against his neck. "In hock to Household Finance up to here."

"Don't you know anyone who could—?"

"No," he sighed. "If I was a sharp chick like you I'd have lots of . . . friends."

She pretended to study the Budweiser label. "A person can always use a friend."

119

Louie smiled and leaned forward. Jenny's breath quickened. No one would be back for at least two hours. Maybe Louie would make an offer. Maybe she would take him up on it. She swung her ankle in small circles. All at once a shadow crossed the carpet. An old man held the leash of a husky wearing a harness and stared in at Louie while the dog sniffed the base of the stop sign. Louie looked at the man, then at the TV, then slapped the arm of the chair and struggled to this feet. "This is one weird setup." He stretched and yawned. "Guess I'll be getting on upstairs."

Jenny cleared her throat to make sure no disappointment caught in her voice. "Things will be back to normal after the remodeling," she said.

"I wonder," he said, and turned towards the doorway.

Before she could get her mind off Louie, Harry Thompson's voice skittered through her memory. "You, Stel, and your aunt live from one nutty scheme to the next." He was probably referring to Jenny's hope that someday he and his wife would split up for good.

Stella only saw Harry once after Jenny confessed he was married. "Bum," Stella yelled, waving a butcher knife over his head as he ran out the door.

Jenny hadn't believed her until near the end of the six-year affair. "Two women fussing over me, I love it," Harry laughed. Jenny wasn't sorry when he and his wife decided to start over in Pittsburgh. Yet she often wondered if the end of the Harry story might have been different if she lived with a sister who ran a Hallmark shop and who talked English right.

So much for Louie, too, Jenny thought, turning out the kitchen light.

The next afternoon, Jenny stood beside her sister in the back room of the store. A dead rat in a trap lay on the butcher-block table. Its gray lips stretched over yellow fangs tipped with blood. A flea crawled along the lavender rim of its ear. "When I loosen this hook," Stella said, "zip out the corpse." Stella popped the spring and a whiff of cheddar drifted from the wooden trap labeled "Victory." Jenny, using the plastic lid, stuffed the tail into a three pound coffee can. Stella tossed the trap back under the table. "We're running low on cans."

"Want to put this body straight in the garbage?"

"We got enough health department violations costing us a fortune in payoffs."

"Sell it to Danny McAllister."

The room suddenly seemed too quiet. Jenny lowered her head, amazed that after all these years the words had slipped out so easily. Outside, a truck lumbered down the alley. The top of the seventh inning blared from a radio. Stella reached into her apron pocket and pulled out a pack of Camels. "Danny who?"

121

Jenny sealed the lid on the can slowly while she recalled how Stella had browbeaten Pa. Although he had been a butcher and a pig farmer in the old country, Pa was scared to death of rats and dreamed they walked around in his mouth. He would wake up screaming there had been four paws with sharp nails on his chest and hot garbagey breath advancing towards his lips. Nothing bothered Stella. So he depended on her to man the traps. When Jenny was about four-teen, she noticed from time to time there would be a rash of dead rats caught mostly in Pa's bed-room, mostly under the head of his bed. With each corpse Pa, a small man anyway, seemed to shrivel up inside himself, while Stella swelled like the dough rising in its greased bowl atop the hot water tank.

"You remember I dated Danny with the Honda?" Jenny asked. Stella held the match horizontally and watched it burn down. "Danny told me when we were in high school he made pin money shooting rats at the docks with his BB gun, then selling them to you. He didn't know why you bought them. But I do." Stella pitched the match into the trash. "Whenever you wanted your way, you stirred up Pa to like he was a zombie with no sleep. He sure knew he needed you."

Stella ran her finger around her Speidel watchband.

"Remember how the rats went away after he bought you the French food processor?" Jenny asked.

Stella walked to the passageway leading to the store, turned, then pointed to the coffee can. "Better bury that before the noon crowd." She added, "Your hands should be fast as your mouth."

The next evening after work, Jenny dragged the suitcase from under her bed. Opening a drawer, she pulled out underwear, still in K mart bags, cut off the price tags, and laid the lingerie on the pink suitcase lining. Then she took out the travel folder. The train schedule was on top. The envelope stamped "Golden Prague Savings and Loan" seemed flat. She looked inside, opened it wider, then tore open the sides as if the ten one-hundred-dollar bills could Gryin a corner. She tossed the envelope on the bed and rummaged through the drawers. Knowing her actions made no sense, she moved the dresser and looked behind it.

Stella. Jenny pictured her flat round face and impassive eyes as she counted bills. Jenny took the steps two at a time.

Stella stood at the stove, one hand on her hip, the other stirring a pot of borscht.

"Where's my money," Jenny shouted.

Stella looked up and raised her eyebrows.

"The cash for my trip. You cleaned me out," Jenny yelled.

Stella stirred faster.

Jenny grabbed Stella's arm. "Hands off,"

she said, then laid the spoon on the table. A scarlet puddle spread over the formica. "Watch this soup while I run down to Santoni's for sour cream." She lifted her sweater from the stove duct. "And watch the lip." Stella sat on the sill, then twisted to push the window open. "Maybe Gryta," she added.

Jenny stood in the center of the room. If Stella was guilty she would never accuse her aunt, Jenny thought. But the old woman had never raided drawers.

Gryta kept her door closed. As Jenny knocked it struck her she hadn't been in this room for some time. "Come inside," Gryta called.

Jenny stared at the walls. Hundreds of comic-paper tulips, roses, gardenias, and lilies from ceiling to baseboard were straight-pinned to the wallpaper. A dusty sunbeam struggled through the torn window blind to fire Prince Valiant's bangs, the silver coil of Mary Worth's chignon, Rex Morgan's scarlet tie. Gryta sat cross-legged in a tattered dentist's chair pasting a clipping in a scrapbook.

"You played my life savings," Jenny said. Gryta bowed her head. "You ought to be locked up."

Jenny steadied herself against the doorjamb to catch her breath. Her eyes rested on the bureau, Gryta's sewing basket overflowing with thimbles of all sizes. When Jenny was a kid, Gryta had patiently taught her how to stitch greeting cards together to make a clipper ship. Gryta had bought Jenny her fist pair of dress-up gloves.

The old woman's arms dropped to her sides like broken wings. Shit, Jenny thought, I can't get the money back, anyway. She walked over and put her arm around the bony shoulders. "Don't mind me."

Gryta smiled, then lowered her face and picked up Jenny's skirt. Folding the hem around her nose she took a deep breath. "I'll get you a hanky," Jenny said. As she hurried from the room the phone rang in the hall and she picked it up.

"This Louie?" a man with a gravely voice asked.

"I'll get him." She laid down the phone and banged on Louie's door. She returned and said, "He's not in. I'll take a message."

"Steve Spassky. Louie can come get the Duster."

Her thoughts raced. "Should I tell Louie if he owes you anything?"

"The grand covers it. Mention I appreciated cash. Slapped it down on the hospital bill as soon as he left."

She dropped the receiver in the cradle, then leaned on the bannister and tried to think. The earthy smell of beet soup rose from the kitchen. She ran downstairs and grabbed the wooden spoon as she passed the table. She swung off the lid and jumped back from the steam.

"Them beets cooking?" Louie sat on the sill and pulled a pack of cigarettes from his breast pocket.

How could she have thought his weaselly eyes and cracked lips were cute?

"Five electricians and I get the dog work," he said, then looked up. "Hey, you mad or something?"

Her knuckles whitened around the wooden handle. She drew back her arm and hurled the spoon at his head. He ducked. It bounced off the wall and clattered to the floor. "Bitch," he yelled.

She blocked his path towards the dining room. "You bought the Duster with my money and I'm calling the cops." She reached for the wall telephone. The police station number was pasted on the dial. Louie's jaw quivered. "You can't prove nothing."

"They'll find fingerprints, question Steve."

Louie's voice dropped. "I never done nothing like this before."

She paused with her hand on the receiver. Why did he admit it right away? Maybe he was such a loser he couldn't imagine not being caught.

"Hey, look," he said eagerly, "Cops don't get no money back." His eyes narrowed. "They just snoop around. Talk to the Health Department."

She dialed the first two digits. He shoved her aside, grabbed the receiver and slammed it down. "Get your hands off me," she yelled.

He raised his right arm, "Swear to God I'll pay back. You don't believe me, take the Duster for collateral."

"I don't want a car," she said wearily.

"I'll sign over the title. Pay you so much a month. If not—hell, maybe you can get more for it. Steve dropped in a new radiator."

She sat at the oak-grained plastic table that shone in the evening sun. Outside, a kid yelled "one-two-three," over and over again. Louie collapsed in the chair across from her. "Thing like this could mess a guy up." He covered his face with his hands. "Everyone else has something going for them. You're all crazy, but going nuts is at least somewhere to go," he said. The kitchen window rattled.

"Eighteen percent interest," Jenny said.

"What's interesting?" Stella asked from the doorway.

"He says he'll pay me back," Jenny said.

Stella's chest swelled. Louie cringed as she leaned over him. Her arms seemed to grow as she reached down and grabbed a handful of knit shirt and yanked Louie half out of the chair.

Suddenly, Jenny imagined Stella stuffing Louie into the cast iron meat grinder, prying his fingers off the greasy lip while his legs twisted around the screwfeeder towards the perforated bottom plate. Next his arms churned down, followed by his neck, a gold tooth. Bone crackled, then Louie appeared, reassembled, sliding whole

127

through the shriveled white casing that hung from the mouth of the grinder. Louie the Lump, sliding towards the knot at the end, his eyes staring at them through the membrane.

"You're hurting me," Louie whimpered.

Stella slammed him down, looked at her hand and wiped it on her apron. "Be out of here in five minutes, bum. And be back in the store first thing tomorrow when we'll get Lawyer Kybczynski to write up a promise note."

Louie, his eyes never leaving Stella, slunk towards the stairs. She ran her finger under her throat.

"Thanks Stel," Jenny whispered.

"For?"

"Sticking up for me."

Stella rubbed her thumb and index finger together. "Blood is sticky."

An hour later, Jenny sat on the edge of her bed. Slowly, she pulled a black slip from the suitcase and stroked the lace. She rose and dropped it into the drawer. Stella's voice came from the hall. "Okay to open?" She stood in the doorway and Jenny was suddenly conscious of the department store bags crumpled in the wastebasket, the cowboy, the empty envelope tossed on the bed. Stella held out her arms and Jenny buried her face in the shoulder that smelled like fried onions. Stella drew back and fumbled in her apron pocket. "Got something." She shoved a roll of bills into Jenny's palm.

"Where's it from?"

"I keep a rainy day."

Jenny's eyes burned. "I can't take it."

Stella put her palm on her heart. "When I was young I should have had more laughing it up, more cowboy." She lifted the hem of her dress and pointed to the varicose veins bulging over her shin. "You think I got these ropes playing golf? But don't worry about me. Take your trip so your heart will be where your feet are."

"Why didn't you want me to go in the first place?"

Stella shrugged. "I'm a dumb hunky worried you might . . ." she flicked her fingers.

Jenny traced the pattern of the doily covering the nightstand. "Remember when I planned to go to the Wild West Show last year?" Jenny asked.

Stella nodded.

"And you had a false alarm heart attack, and I bought the fence?"

Stella nodded again.

"This year I thought you wanted a sign."

Stella pointed to the money. "Sign, schmine. Go."

Jenny held out the bills.

Stella rubbed her palms together. "I got to check the soup. Think it over. And don't worry about the store." She smiled and suddenly Jenny thought of the rat pinned under the spring. "Neon blinkers come and go," Stella said, closing the door softly behind her.

The money felt furry in Jenny's palm. Had Stella given it for power, or for love? Did it matter? If Stella owned the trip, the reason to go was gone. Jenny sat on the bed and folded a crease in the spread. Another year, another vacation shot to hell. Slowly she tucked the bills in her skirt pocket and rose to take them back.

On the landing, she hesitated and drew out the bills. They seemed to throb, as if alive. Why not take them? She could offer to pay Stella back—except Stella, for sure, would refuse, wanting to hang on to her status as the giver rather than the givee. So why not buy into Stella's power trip? If Jenny got to the Grand Canyon, at least this year might go down in history as a draw. Holding onto the bannister she slowly pivoted into the living room on one foot.

In the kitchen, Stella was chopping carrots and Louie leaned over Gryta's shoulder. He looked up, spotted Jenny and said, "I'm going, I'm going," then pointed to his duffle bag under the window. Gryta finished writing something and handed him a scrap of paper. "Will hit next Friday," she said.

He tucked it in his breast pocket. "For sure?"

"The feast day of Saint Gertrude."

He turned to Jenny. "Pay you back Friday."

"Only I won't be here," Jenny said.

Stella's hand stopped midair.

"I'll be in Denver."

Louie shrugged. "See you tomorrow," he

said. "And when my ship comes in." He swung his leg over the sill.

Stella tossed a carrot onto the drainboard. "Ships always sink."

"Oh, no they don't," Gryta said, adjusting a Rex Morgan daisy behind her ear. "They splash, bubble, make waves, then swim straight into the sun like fish, never touching ground."

EIGHT

Persecution Is for You

Although I am a friend of the Kostick family and Monsignor of their parish, I cannot recall serving as confessor to Joseph or his son, Pavel. Therefore, I am not violating the seal of the Sacrament by telling you what happened to Pavel in the twin city to Nazareth.

Pavel and I photograph birds, an interest shared since he was a boy. The Saturdays I'm free from parish affairs, we roam the cliffs above the Chesapeake Bay. The story he told was far more than an episode in the life of a troubled young man. It illustrates how poisons simmer in the mind. How did I know what was in Pavel's heart? Men are not so different from one another. God gave us a finite number of themes, and I know them all. Hum a few bars, and I'll play you the tune. I have the gift of empathy, you see, the voice and vision of one man felt through the lips and eyes of another.

Joseph Kostick paid little attention to his son. Pavel told me sometimes he wished he could fly into his father's head and shout, "Talking to you is talking to a stone." I could have warned Pavel the old man wouldn't listen. A stone turned inside-out is still a stone.

At twenty-two Pavel was the youngest artist to be commissioned by our Baltimore Archdiocese. I remember the morning Pavel's painting, "Persecution," was unveiled over the font in the Hospice of Saint Anne. I, my Associate Pastor, even Bishop Novak came out to see the magnificent oil. But only a few of us and Pavel's father would have recognized Pavel's mother in the eyes of Saint Joan. And Joseph had not come. At the reception Pavel slipped away from the crowd around the punch bowl.

Some months later, Pavel and I sat on our favorite grassy bluff overlooking the bay. Halfway down, a dead tree supported an osprey's nest. The wonderful birds were away from Maryland this time of year. The empty nest was ragged as a mangled broom, yet our eyes clung to the straw. Much of Pavel's discourse was of an intimate nature. Therefore, we pretended we were merely passing time until the birds soared before our lens.

Pavel told me he had left the reception enraged. Home, he strapped his knapsack on the back of his Harley Davidson and took off without speaking to his father, Joseph. On his way out of town he stopped at a banking machine to withdraw the balance of his account. He said he planned to pick up a job in a lumber yard or fish for salmon when he got to the West Coast—a romantic ambition considering Pavel's physique. Unlike Joseph, a robust man with arms like derricks, Pavel was spindly, his blond beard a spider web. Blue veins showed under the skin on his temples. Some frail men achieve distinction by elegance of carriage. Pavel cringed.

On his trip west, Pavel had expected to make Pittsburgh before dark. But somewhere past Cumberland the bike started to burn oil and an hour later the engine quit. He was stranded in a shabby town spread across the slope of Mt. Sorry-Dog. I pointed out he was lucky to have found a gas station. Pavel suggested I try squatting on a pile of oil cans, watching my Buick engine swing from a hoist.

A kestrel whirled above the beach where Pavel and I sat, and I turned my attention from the osprey's nest. "What was the name of the town where you were stranded?" I asked him.

Pavel answered, "This guy, Dwayne, is monkeying around with the block. He says, "Shackle, West Virginia, boy. Twin city to Nazareth.""

Without a car-rental or motel nearby, Pavel had admitted he traded Dwayne his last dime shooter of cocaine for a ride and a place to sleep. Pavel, who usually lacked stamina, had been exhausted. He remembers wanting a cold beer and what he called a joint, actually a poisonous weed, and wondered how much worse his luck could get. Of course Pavel blamed his predicament, as he did everything, on his father. None of this would have happened if Joseph had gone to the unveiling of Pavel's painting. He had been invited. Pavel had even left a photo of "Persecution," featured in *The Baltimore Sun*, on his father's desk. Later, Pavel had spotted the clipping beside the wastebasket on the rug.

Nothing Pavel did pleased the old man. I recall when Pavel won a scholarship. Pavel, not his father, told me about his honors award. Joseph only said to Pavel that they did not need the money.

But Joseph's indifference to "Persecution" had devastated the boy. In moments of grandeur, Pavel believed this to be the first of his paintings that would alter the history of art, immortalize the Kostick name. The father should have been proud of his son. Though I am quite fond of Joseph, and respect his skill and reputation as a surgeon, I must admit that I consider him a misanthrope.

Even as a young man Joseph preferred an ocean between himself and his people. When he was twenty he had emigrated from Prague. Joseph told me he left because he could no longer stand the stone eyes of the statues hewn into every entablature in the city. Madonnas, enraged archangels, a crazed Zeus with bared teeth staring down the back of his overcoat. Grainy eyes watched from cornices and judged, judged him blowing his nose in the Vlatava River, judged him with a girl in Mala Strana park.

In America, Joseph had worked his way through medical school as a longshoreman at the McCormick pier. Each dawn he loaded tea into the holds of those tankers with rusty water dripping like tobacco juice from their portholes. He rented a room above Charlie Mikalauskas' bakery, and boiled cabbage and white bacon on a hotplate. At the end of his residency he was offered a post at Johns Hopkins Hospital. Perhaps hoping to end the habits of an isolated man, Joseph had married Sophie Mikalauskas, Charlie's fragile, blond niece. Pavel was born soon after they bought the Victorian mansion in Roland Park. Five years later Sophie died of leukemia.

But returning to Pavel stranded in Shackle, he described the inside of Dwayne's pickup truck. The dashboard was cluttered with mementos. I expressed interest in Pavel's description of a plastic coin embossed with a profile of Oral Roberts that hung from the rear-view mirror. I knew Pavel was teasing me when he said, "Ecumenicism, man."

Pavel also described the ride with Dwayne to his sister's house. I can picture the TV satellite beside the woodpile, condensation trickling from the spokes inside those giant bowls that look like umbrellas propped to dry.

Pavel's attraction to Dwayne's sister had been instant. Apparently, Eva was a handsome woman. But I believe Pavel was drawn to a quality he attempted to explain, her aura of independence, competence. He described her black hair worn in long braids. He observed, as an artist would, that too many bones seemed to frame her jaw, wrists, tan cheeks and shoulders.

Pavel remarked that he had never been inside so modest a home. He recalled a sagging double bed in the center of the living room, and a television set that rested on a refrigerator that hummed in the corner. Pavel was to spend the night in Eva's house, while Dwayne and his girlfriend shared a trailer across the road. Dwayne had assured Pavel before he left that he would return in the morning and drive him to Cumberland for a rebuilt engine.

The shabby furnishings, the smell of foods fried in dirty fat, these things unnerved Pavel. Good, I say. Pavel spent his youth in shopping malls. It was time for him to learn the world as a sorry place indeed.

Eva offered to make dinner, and opened a can of USDA commodity butter. Pavel recalled she had peeled off one circle of bologna, then counted the slices left in the package. I caught a note of sympathy, but also superiority in his voice. An old woman, who apparently lived with Eva, leaned on a cane and held up a macramè rope. Pavel imitated her, "For hangy-down plants. I done it at the Golden Years," he said.

I admonished Pavel for his unkindness. He picked up his zoom lens and studied the trees around the osprey nest. I restrained my urge to borrow the glass, a thousand-dollar German import, and he went on with his story.

"Sorry Father, you're not connecting with the scene. See, Eva passes me this sandwich and it's on a paper towel. You know what was under the sink where the dishwasher should be? A doghouse. Probably no dishes, either. Then it hits me she made one sandwich so I ask her where hers is and she ducks her head behind a cabinet, making me feel like shit."

Pavel cleared his throat and I pretended not to hear his last word. We Dominicans can honor a word, or dismiss it at will. He told me he had affected a casual manner and invited her out for a pizza. I praised Pavel for the gesture which was considerate and tactful. But she told him she had already eaten. He must have forced down that sandwich just as he had forced down dinner as a child.

During the past twenty years, I have dined at the Kostick home on the first Thursday of each month. I recall many dinners when Pavel was a boy. Joseph, wearing a smoking jacket, had presided over the long Hepplewhite table. His oily eyelids hung like half-lowered warehouse doors over his black eyes. Every few minutes, he would spear a spool of kielbasa from the soup with a paring knife, then bite the meat off the tip. I remember the clink of the vodka bottle against Joseph's glass as he refilled it, and the housekeeper shuffling in the kitchen. Joseph and I would discuss the Baltimore Orioles. If Pavel dared to speak, Joseph turned his head away.

Pavel continued his story. Eva had gone to work and had left Pavel with the old woman, who had lain on the bed watching a plane rise from a jungle airstrip on television. The sight of the P-51 stirred up Pavel's anger at his father all over again.

Joseph, you see, built fighter planes as a hobby, then hung them on wires from the ceiling throughout his house. Although I say hobby, obsession is the better word. In the beginning, Joseph had explained that wiring the propellers and tying the tiny knots maintained his surgical dexterity. Later it became apparent that the planes were his greatest, perhaps only, pleasure. In the Kostick mansion, shadows of F-14s and Mustangs drifted over the burled tables and Aubusson rugs like black crosses. Pavel loathed those giant, circling insects. He once told me they judged his every move.

Pavel and the old woman had watched the end of the movie, then she had led him to a bedroom, where he had unrolled his sleeping bag on the floor. He awoke when Dwayne's slurred voice answered by Eva's murmurs echoed from downstairs. He realized he must have dozed, for the next thing he recalled was Eva leaning over him. She had shoved a gun between his ribs and

the bag and asked him to hide it, putting her
finger over her lips and whispering that Dwayne
was high and wanted to kill his girlfriend and
that the gun was loaded.

The next morning Pavel had found Dwayne
asleep on the sofa. He would not get up. Desperate to resume his trip, Pavel had coaxed Eva into
driving him to Cumberland to get the rebuilt
engine. She had agreed to find another waitress
to cover for her at the diner.

Pavel described Eva's hair, that day braided
into one long plait. He said her shirt could have
been Dwayne's. Her blue jeans were taut across
the skulls of her knees. The long drive had
afforded him the opportunity to tell her about
his life. He had told her about Joseph, his
mother, and he had reminisced about his grand-
parents. Sometimes people believe they can elicit
more sympathy from strangers than from friends
who have witnessed their failings.

I visited the Mikalauskas family often, in
their East Baltimore row-house with lilies
painted on the screen door and marble steps
worn round at the edges. They welcomed me as
they did everyone. There was always an accordian playing, and someone on the daybed in the
club cellar recovering from a hangover. I was
often struck by the sharp contrast between the
cold world Joseph seemed to create around him
and the warmth of the Mikalauskas' home. I had
hoped that contrast would have prevented Pavel
from becoming too much like his father.

I recall one party that lasted two days. I, of course, only stopped for an hour or so. Pavel, waiting for company, was dressed in a newspaper Indian suit his grandmother cut, and dashing back and forth between the front window and the kitchen. Grandpa Mikas had fired up the coal burner and the fiberglass drapes billowed like spinnakers over the living room radiators. In the kitchen, Pavel's grandmother had poured whiskey and cherry pop into glasses decorated with decals of bird hunters. I must say the cherry was a tangy complement to the scotch.

Then the doorbell clanged. Josie Jogalis stood on the stoop. She was one of the few Baltimore Lithuanians successful in real estate. A mink coat slid from one shoulder as she waved a patent leather pocketbook that bulged with a fifth of Four Roses. Vera Rapalis stood behind her. Charlie Crow followed Vito Rapalis into the vestibule that smelled like cabbage and was as hot as a Bessemer furnace.

By midnight Mike was playing "The Happy Vilnius Polka" on his accordian for the third time. Charlie Crow hopped onto the buffet, flapped his elbows and cackled like a rooster while Mikas strode through the crowd swinging the old gray tomcat. He tossed the animal on the chandelier above the dining room table. The cat rode the pitching armature until it slowed, then leaped over the tray of steaming perogies onto the floor. All the while, Joseph slumped in a corner, a glass in one hand, vodka bottle in the other. Sweat glistened on his sullen face. When his bottle was empty, he staggered into the living room and passed out on the couch.

This party took place about five months before poor Sophie died. I remember watching the pretty young woman as she sat with her feet thrust towards the gas fire. Her plate, untouched, had rested on the arm of her chair. Mikas had waved a butcher knife over her cold potato pancakes and shouted, "Eat, eat. Look how you look!" Sophie had smiled, then glanced at Joe's empty chair and stiffened.

Pavel and I have often debated whether Joseph was nasty or just indifferent.

Pavel told me that he and Eva had arrived in Cumberland too late; the dealership was closed. Eva suggested that the next day they get an earlier start, but Pavel was never one for patience. He urged her to stay in the Holiday Inn they had just passed. When she hesitated he assured her he could afford two rooms. She remained reluctant explaining she did not have things like pajamas. He offered to lend her a T-shirt.

Admittedly, the next part of the story is a bit hazy. I hope I did not offend Pavel by questioning him closely. My interest was not prurient. Professionally, I must from time to time delve into circumstances that illustrate the scope of human error and the folly of passion.

Eva's motel room had been no doubt like

one of those I rent while attending various conferences and seminars. Steam always clouds a mirror framed in simulated renaissance oak. Pavel had come to her room to give her his T-shirt. She probably held the shirt against her shoulders to see if it fit. Pavel had pointed out the garment was hardly Dior, and she told him she bought her clothing at the Union Mission. He said she deserved red silk with seed pearls and 14-carat threads, then embraced her. Again, I commended Pavel for his consideration.

His next words, "I love you," were not well chosen.

Naturally, she had not believed him.

For some reason, perhaps the anxiety that accompanies lust, Pavel had felt it essential to convince her. He told her they could leave for Seattle tomorrow. Or go to San Francisco.

Again she did not believe him. He said they would marry and live on Telegraph Hill. She told him people do not marry anymore. This surprised me greatly. Then according to Pavel she began to comb her hair and berate him at the same time. She said he was turning their arrangement into a lie in order to make himself look good. I believe I understand the gist of her thoughts. Pavel's grand delusions had made the tawdry situation ridiculous as well.

Pavel, probably desperate, had looked around the room as if he could find a substitute for words. Inspired, he had scooped his wallet off the room service menu, telling her to forget the Union Mission, to buy whatever she wanted. He said he had pulled out a handful of cash and folded it into her palm.

Sometimes I believe Pavel expressed genuine goodwill. He did not intend to compromise Eva. Although the consummation of their encounter seemed imminent without barter, I suspect Pavel preferred to buy her affections. Perhaps his unattractive image of himself, unfortunately correct, caused him to believe purchase was the only secure route to love.

He described how Eva had jumped away from him and had tucked the bills into the breast pocket of the shirt she was wearing.

He remembers smiling and holding out his arms.

She told him to get out.

At this point in his story, Pavel's eyes left the osprey's nest. He turned to me and said, "I only wanted to give her something. What did I do wrong?"

I uncorked my thermos of strong Lychee tea and passed it to Pavel. "Did you ask Eva?"

Pavel nodded.

I held my china cup and saucer—I carry these with me at all times—in one hand and with the other I poured my tea. I held the cup aloft to savor the fragrance of blossoms. Not as sweet as jasmine, but herbal, a hint of Oolong. "What did she say?"

He repeated her exact words to me. " 'Don't give me that shit. You did it for you. I didn't even want your goddamn pizza.' "

"Then what?" I asked.

"She jockeys me into the hall and slams the door," he said.

Poor Pavel. I can imagine how foolish he felt standing in the corridor. He remembered the elevator bell rang and voices echoed from the stairwell. He had rapped on Eva's door and yelled at her to give back the money and had heard the dead bolt click into place.

He rang her room until the desk clerk complained. The next morning, he convinced the cleaning woman to unlock Eva's door. Of course she was no longer there.

In his room he had flung himself across the bed. If he had offended Eva, Eva with so much pride, where was the money?

I thought Pavel had a point, but I did not tell him that. It would be unkind to suggest that he is not the sort to attract pretty girls unless they have evil motives.

But consider Eva. She did not exactly steal. A rich man might as well pay for the privilege of playing the fool.

Pavel told me that while he stared at the ceiling in that dismal room, he had convinced himself that Eva had set him up and that Dwayne was an accomplice. Joseph's rejection, Eva's rejection, grew larger in Pavel's mind. A tree of paranoia can spring from one seed of truth. Pavel had convinced himself that Eva, Dwayne and Joseph only wanted what they could take from him. Although it was not entirely clear to me what Pavel thought they wanted.

Pavel had also regretted his lack of foresight and courage to retrieve the money before Eva shut the door. He hated himself for being what he called a wimp.

Then he realized he was trapped in Cumberland. He said he had jumped out of bed and checked his wallet. There was a credit card and enough cash for a few weeks. He could hitch a ride to Shackle carrying the rebuilt engine, then be back on the road to Seattle. Maybe he would get a chance to settle up with Eva. But there could be difficulties with Dwayne. The forces assailing Pavel overwhelmed him. He told me that he stumbled to the bathroom, unwrapped a glass and washed down two Dexedrine capsules, an understandable mistake, but a mistake.

He checked out of the motel. Ten o'clock and already the streets were on fire. Pavel had tried to recall where the dealership was. He made a wrong turn and walked along streets lined with two-story frame houses, that section of town where strips of peeling paint hang like flypaper from the weathered cornices. Pavel had seen the slim windows as eyes, plotting against him from octagonal turrets. He had wiped his brow and pushed through a flock of old women descending from a bus, sweaters swinging over their shoulders. They had straggled into an abandoned factory, now a glassware outlet. Pavel had paused before a display of crystal in the sunlit window. Suddenly, and to this day he insists, he smelled turpentine. He cupped his hands around his eyes and studied a Victorian bowl. Eva's face was dissolving inside, the black of her hair graying her cheeks.

From this point on, Pavel's memory was unclear. He recalls feeling delirious, moving as if in a dream. His stomach had cramped as the drug took effect. He had found a bathroom in a gas station. Back on the sidewalk, the store fronts and telegraph poles blurred into layers of chrome yellow. He said he thought of the yellow robe the monk wore in "Jesuit," the half-finished canvas on his easel. It had struck him that the light from a stained-glass window in the upper corner was wrong. All at once, he had to find a church to study a sunbeam filtered through red glass. I know better. His mother had worn a Crucifix on a silver chain around her throat. "To chase werewolves?" Joseph had asked. "Of course," she had replied. Pavel was chasing his devil with a Cross.

Someone had directed Pavel to Saint Luke's. Pavel said he ran across the bridge. He could almost smell the incense that would, as he put it, mellow his nerves, hear the kneeling-plank thump against the stone floor and echo to the top of a vaulted ceiling. He could rest in the glorious light warming the brow of the pew in front of him, the painter's golden light scored by marble pillars.

I am embarrassed to recount the following

incident, the slippage that has occurred in our haste to achieve the promise of the Second Vatican Council. I believe that an aerial view of America would reveal a national tract development of hideous new churches, Saint Luke's a prototype. I am familiar with the building as I attended the Ecumenical Leaders Group Retreat in the basement. The sign on the front lawn reads, "God wants a Meaningful Relationship." The roof of the one-story masonry structure is a fiberglass triangle. The door handle is a giant vertical staple affixed to an orange metal door. I do not blame the boy for turning away. I myself could hardly bear to step inside. I cannot begin to tell you all the ugly details; the recessed lights, the indoor-outdoor carpet, the statue of Our Lady with the face of a suburban housewife, the atonal choir selections. I could go on.

Again, Pavel was betrayed. The church became a symbol of all the ugliness that had soured his life. He said he fled from Saint Luke's. Despite the heat, his teeth chattered. He sat on the curb, opened his knapsack, and reached for his vial of Seconal. Something metal blocked his hand. He had almost forgotten the gun wrapped in his underwear. Not daring to take it out on the street, he stroked the embossed handle.

I hear Pavel's thoughts as if they were my own. What if I point this at Eva? No, better the old man. For once he will pay attention. Or will he? He will if I pull the trigger.

Pavel, driven by thwarted pride, frustrated passion, chemicals, had reached the depth of despair.

"Kill my father." There was no emotion in Pavel's voice as he said these words. A fresh breeze kicked up whitecaps on the bay. Pavel shielded his eyes. "I freaked out," he said.

I detected a note of arrogance or of pride. Perhaps, because he was a coward, the pride was only of a courageous thought. But I could be too tolerant of Joseph's son. There are men who do not know the difference between right and wrong. Further, they lack the capacity to learn the difference once explained. I wondered if my young friend was one of them.

Pavel remembers swallowing another drug capsule without water, and heading towards the Greyhound station. He had to wait several hours for the bus to Baltimore. He bought coffee and added six packets of sugar to compensate for the breakfast he had missed.

He recalls very little of the ride. The roar of the motor lulled him into a stupor. From Cumberland to Hancock he slumped with his forehead pressed against the window. I can see the interstate signs—Indian Spring, Clearwater, Hagerstown, Frederick—blurring into waves as green as those lapping the shore at our feet.

Curious, how events coincide. While Pavel headed home, I too was on my way to the Kostick house. It was the first Thursday of the month, when I usually dined with Joseph. I left the rectory early in order to buy a bottle of Malaga. There is only one store in the city that carries this marvelous wine. Bottle under my arm, I set out for the long trek up Charles Street. I felt obligated to exercise before enjoying Joseph's fine table. Near the entrance to Roland Park, a parishioner pulled up beside me in his jeep. I was grateful for the ride to Joseph's house. I am not lazy, but was interested in the vehicle.

Pavel's bus arrived in Baltimore at six o'clock. He recalls stumbling onto Howard Street. He kept bumping into shoppers from Lexington Market hugging their bags, which for some reason are always topped with celery leaves. The glare from the sidewalk hurt Pavel's eyes so he hailed a taxi.

Pavel must have arrived about fifteen minutes ahead of me. The driver dropped him off at the foot of the Kostick driveway, which was guarded by two marble gryphons. Pavel unlocked the door but forgot to close it. The foyer was cool and quiet. He recalls that for the first time in his life, he looked directly at the wooden airplanes. Their nacelles met his eyes. He headed towards the open stairway that rises from the living room to the landing. He remembers clinging to the bannister to steady himself.

Often I have visited Joseph in his attic. Oak branches brushing the eaves keep the room in darkness. The vast dormered space is lit only by the gooseneck lamp on Joe's workbench under the opened window. Joseph collected old theater seats and had Jeremy, his yard boy, bolt them in a semicircle behind the workbench. He had given me one with baroque carving.

Pavel lowered his knapsack beside the red velvet empire chair with rosettes carved on the arms. Joseph, his back to the door, sat on his high stool, his aviator scarf in its usual place, dangled from the caned back. Sections of fringe hung in spears that Joseph had wrought between his thumb and fingers. Joseph's summer costume for working around the house was the top to a union suit and plaid bermudas that reached to his shiny white knees. He has become decidedly smaller, as I do with age. Muscles that once bulged now creep from the bone. Pavel said he must have made a sound, for Joseph turned.

At about that time, I was crossing the porch. I was early, but reasoned that Joseph and I could linger over drinks. The opened door disturbed me. I rapped, and stepped into the foyer. The house was quiet, then I heard voices coming from upstairs. I did not wish to intrude, but I had to be certain a robbery was not taking place. I gripped the neck of the bottle and crept toward the landing. I heard Joseph say, "You have been traveling," with his slight "k" sound on the "g."

"To the twin city to Nazareth," Pavel's voice replied.

I was embarrassed, afraid I would be caught and misunderstood. I held my breath, and slowly, very slowly for I could have tripped, I backed down the stairs.

From his tone I suspect a smile in Joseph's voice, "Nazareth. Where His own spurned Him."

I paused, intrigued, imagining Joseph peering over his wire-rimmed glasses as he always does to survey the workbench, then selecting a surgical tool to construct his planes.

Pavel's voice shook, "You should have gone to the unveiling."

"I didn't have to," Joseph replied.

Pavel sounded more grandiose than usual. "I layered that canvas with the soul of us."

I can see Joseph lifting a propeller blade the size of a paper clip.

Pavel shouted, " 'Persecution' was for you."

Joseph's voice was mocking, "It is for you, Pavel."

I fought the urge to laugh. Indeed, persecution may be the destiny of Pavel. I was careful not to drop the bottle as I took another step backwards. To this day neither Pavel nor Joseph knows that I overheard their words. I retreated to the lower hall. I planned to pretend I had found the door open and assumed Joseph was upstairs, and that I waited for him to come down.

Pavel told me how the old man's back was to him. He said he tried to keep his hand steady as he drew the pistol from his knapsack. Joseph reached to adjust the lamp and Pavel said suddenly the room spun and he was confronted with a vision. The hairs on Joseph's head became dandelion fuzz, fragile and white. Before Pavel's eyes, Joseph shriveled, turned into a pod of seeds, all that remained of the stiff spokes of the yellow wheel. Pavel's aim blurred. At that moment, he grasped what I had been telling him for years. Nothing he could do to the old man would matter. Pavel said he saw the imaginary bullet whizzing straight through the pod, then out the window. His father would turn and say, "'Persecution' is for you."

Pavel recalls shoving the weapon back into his knapsack. One last time he tried to get Joseph's attention. I heard Pavel shout, "God damn."

Pavel said the old man turned and waved his arm in dismissal.

I was standing in the dining room pretending to admire a portrait of Lord Calvert. You can imagine my surprise when Pavel dashed past me. I came up behind him but something in his stance prevented me from speaking. He stared at the ceiling. The shadow of the F8F Bearcat slid across the table. Then he strode into the living room, and gazed up at the Airacobra twisting over the piano. I watched him lift the gun from his bag and aim.

I was about to cry out, then I understood. I stepped back. The shot cracked and the pistol jumped in his hand exploding splinters over the sofa. Only winging a B-14, he circled back and split the bright blue star on the fuselage. He steadied himself against the desk while he picked off the Mustang that pitched in the doorway. A khaki wing tip landed in a bowl of waterlilies. Pavel licked his cracked lips and studied the smoking gun. Wires, shimmering like rungs of broken cobwebs, dangled from the ceiling. Instead of a shadow, a wheel the size of a button rested on the burled writing table.

Footsteps shuffled on the stairs. Pavel gazed around the room as if this would be the last time he would see it.

Suddenly, I felt eyes upon me. Pavel and I looked up at the same time. Joseph stood on the second floor landing. He leaned and rested his arms on the bannister, then adjusted his glasses on the bridge of his nose.

Pavel glanced at his feet. When he raised his head, his father was gone. I, the intruder, remained silent. Slowly, Pavel walked out the front door and slammed it behind him.

Trembling from an emotion I cannot name, I wiped my brow. Something on the floor caught my eye. I stooped and lifted a tiny plastic aviator from the lavender carpet. The man's knees were bent to the contour of a pilot's seat. A jagged seam ridged the crest of his helmet. The man's mouth was slightly open. His smile curled from one goggle strap to another; bright red, too wide, a flaw in the mold.

I walked to the porch. Joseph and I would dine another night. Then I turned back. In the foyer, I placed the Malaga on a shelf beneath a mirror.

NINE

Knights of Puntukas

You think because I am an old woman just off the boat, so to speak, I don't know what happened to Zappardino and my brotherhood? Take that back. Not mine. The Knights of Puntukas is men only. I'm the auxiliary, partly because I speak and write in English as well as Lithuanian, and partly because I'm best friends with the Grand Master, Constantine Skupas.

The Knights are organizing a crusade to win back the Holy Land. Connie says Jerusalem is where our Church was born and so it has to be under the Pope's thumb. Boy though, would you be surprised at the number of people who don't agree. Even Father Abrovaitas says Connie Skupas is all wet.

This Zappardino business started last May. Every month we Knights get together in the back of Novotsky's Bar and Grill. Novotsky charges big money for meeting space, but where else in East Baltimore can a person get potato kugelis, homemade. The back room is behind the ladies' entrance and is hidden by a gold curtain.

Being the owner-operator of the Queen-O-Clean Laundromat, I can't get away until six. As usual I got to the back room just in time to hang the banner and check the ice buckets, the folding chairs, and Novotsky's slippery fingers. Connie buys the vodka—Stolichnaya only. Last month the bottles on the serving tray had been unscrewed. "Convenience," said Novotsky, his fox face all smiles.

One by one the Knights came in. It's always touch-and-go as to whether we get a quorum. Magas, the wizard, leaning on his stick, stopped every minute to catch his breath. Geminaikas was followed by Vito with his cousin Stan at his heels. Joe, who always kids around, took one look at my new pink cardigan and wolf whistled. To celebrate the results of my current diet I had gotten my hair touched up and set Nancy Reagan style. Louie, Petronas, and Radas found seats, while outside Connie paced up and down the sidewalk so he could be a minute late. At 7:10 our Grand Master swung aside the curtain and everyone stood. Connie is short, skinny, and seventy-five years old. But he walks like a king. For meetings he drapes a red scarf around his shoulders and pins it to his jacket with his solidarity button.

The ceremonies started with Joe saying a prayer, then the Knights singing the Lithuanian National Anthem and the Star Spangled Banner. We sat down and waited for Magas to read the famous poem. Each meeting he recites how the devil was about to drop Puntukas Rock on the village of Anykščiai when the Angel of the Lord kicked the rock aside and the people were saved. Magas' beard covered his chest like a nest of cobwebs. For the Knights and other special occasions he wears a white linen vest embroidered with a Sūduva Cross in red sequins. The long vest hangs to his knees so you can only see the frayed bottoms of his pants. I sat beside Connie and after a few minutes I noticed he was twisting his ruby ring around and around on his finger. When Magas spread his arms to show the size of the sacred oaks, Connie jerked back and frowned. Just mentioning Puntukas usually made his eyes water, but that night Connie squinted at the air as if the beautiful words were gnats. Something was eating him.

I delivered the minutes of the April meeting, then the treasurer's report. Our membership drive had been a roaring success. Everyone had paid me five dollars a year, cash on the barrelhead, and after expenses we still had fifty bucks. Connie lifted his glass and mumbled a half-hearted "Sveikas." We all shouted, "I Sveikata," and drank up. I hardly had time to finish before Connie announced it was time for the Grand Master's report. He pulled a letter from the pocket of his orange blazer and handed it to me. Before reading it aloud I explained it was the answer to our petition to the Pope asking for seven thousand dollars for a feasibility study.

Considering diplomacy and all the cold wars, this crusade would be tricky to pull off. Connie convinced us that before the Vatican would finance the expedition, we needed a foolproof plan. The Pope is a man of vision, Connie said. And certainly would float the research for a mission that would change the destiny of the world. Seven thousand would be just enough to hire a high-class consulting firm. As Connie put it, experts are for thinking, Knights are for the real McCoy.

The Pope was polite and blessed us for our opinions. Only there was no mention of the seven thousand, or the crusade. The seal looked official, but I bet it was the same letter for everybody printed on a word machine. His Holiness had enclosed an oval medal with his face carved on one side. Connie waited until the gist of the letter sank in, then said, "That is why I, myself, must go to Rome and explain everything."

I was knocked flat. Neither Connie nor I had ever exactly married so we were, you might say, each other's family. Yet he hadn't sprung this one on me. Magas carefully turned his stick propped against the table. Louie picked at a loose button on his overall bib. Joe, helping himself to a vodka refill, said, "No way. Air fare alone must cost a thousand dollars."

Connie tipped his hand back and forth. "Eight hundred, give or take. That includes one week hotel."

Vito whistled.

"And yet," Geminaikas said slowly, "Wouldn't face to face with our Little Father be best?"

"We're seven hundred fifty dollars short," I pointed out.

Petronas turned to me and said, "Okay Maruta, forget the Holy Land. Staying home is dirt cheap."

He was right. Every crusader worth his salt must have had money problems, and we had to solve ours. How about a bake sale I was about to ask before I remembered who would bake. "We could raffle off a new car."

"We don't have a new car," Vito said.

Connie rubbed his shot glass as if it were a worry stone instead. "There is a way," he said slowly. Faces turned towards him. "Dom Zappardino offered to stake me."

Zappardino's house is a block down from mine. It's a two-family red brick job, with a red brick wall along the sidewalk, a red brick porch, and square red brick planters like bookends against the front steps. I pictured Dominic, short, fat, former mason, now owner of East Baltimore's fastest growing real estate operation. I opened my mouth to ask what's in it for him, and Connie held up his hand. "There's a catch."

The Knights leaned forward.

"I have to get Zapp's incorporation papers blessed by His Holiness," Connie said, then added, "He's scared his business will fall flat on its face."

"Then let him fly to Rome," I said.

"Zapp said his wife would want to go, and where Mafalda goes the twins go, and Constanza, and no-good Jimmy, and Aunt Aida, who all her life prayed to visit Saint Peters, just once."

Joe laughed and slapped the table. "So we get a face-to-face and Zappardino gets off cheap."

Geminaikas looked at the ceiling and mumbled "Thank you."

My mind was going a mile a minute. "Not so fast," I said. "Remember, Zapp's just bought the vacant lot next to Saint Casimer's. The blessing will help him put up that entertainment arcade everybody's predicting."

After a silence Petronas said, "Pizza takeouts. Waxi-Maxis."

"Punk rockers," Geminaikas said.

Louie's large bony hands shook. "Video games within earshot of the Holy Eucharist."

Petronas ran his fingernail down the Stolichnaya label and dropped the coil in an ashtray. "We can raise our own money."

"Would take us one hundred years," Connie said.

Joe shrugged. "We got time."

"The Pope needs the Church of the Holy Sepulcher," Connie said, making a fist. "Now."

"Gethsemane, too," Radas said quietly.

The Knights argued this way and that way. Finally Joe said, "Look, if God wants an arcade He'll build an arcade. Connie's a messenger for a blessing, that's all."

Why hadn't I thought of that? Whether a blessing took or not was beyond our business.

Magas raised his head. A silver thread of beard was caught on a sequin, a spider's work. "Suppose the devil wants the arcade?"

Petronas looked thoughtful. "Whoever wants it bothered to put it into Zapp's head to send Connie to Rome."

"Why?" I asked.

The room went quiet again. Finally Connie said, "Could be God's teaching us how to cut deals."

"What deals?" I asked.

He went on, "Look at it this way. In the old country we were beet farmers. America is a land of opportunities."

"Of Zappardinos," Geminaikas muttered.

"My point exactly," Connie said.

Now I saw what he was driving at and most of the Knights were nodding too. With his thumb and index finger Magas flattened his beard beneath his chin.

Right then Irena Novotsky waddled in carrying a skillet by its handle wrapped in a dishtowel. The room suddenly smelled of fried pork and bay leaf. The kugelis, garnished with onions, bubbled in bacon fat. The Zappardino decision could not be put off. I turned to Connie. "What should we do?"

Connie looked at the potatoes, then at the Puntukas banner tacked on the wall. It showed a Knight on horseback wearing a vest like Magas'. The dome of Jerusalem shone in the distance. Up in the sky, Osier, the adder king, was coiled to spell the word, "Musti," strike. Osier's head was the top of the letter "i". Instead of a dot there was a tiny crown, snake's head size.

"Play along," Connie said.

Two weeks later, Connie, Magas and I waited in the airport for Connie's flight to New York. The Knights agreed I should drive to save taxi fare. Magas came for the ride. We stood under the television flight schedule that hung from the ceiling. A group of ladies wearing hats and pantsuits gathered around their tour leader. A boy with a knapsack on his back sat on an airline animal cage. Inside a hamster chewed on the bars. Suddenly a little girl, hugging a giant stuffed Mickey Mouse, pointed to Magas's vest and yelled, "Why's that man in dress?" Every head turned to Magas and the mother dragged the kid onto the main concourse.

"Got your itinerary, Zapp's papers, and the letter from the Archbishop?" I asked.

Boy, the trouble it took to get Father Abrovaitas to contact the Archbishop to write to

the Maestro di Camera who arranges papal
audiences. I convinced Father that even if he
didn't believe in the crusade there was no harm
in humoring Connie. And when—Father said
"if"—we pulled it off, the Archbishop would get
some of the thanks. On the bright side, Father
said the Archbishop and the Maestro had once
served on a Liturgical Renewal Committee, so
Connie shot off his mouth that getting in to see
the Pope would be a snap. The night before last,
Joe lugged a case of champagne to my place and
I boiled enough kielbasa and cabbage to feed an
army. The Knights throw parties at the drop of a
hat. Sometimes I wonder how many believe in
the crusade or how many just go along for the
social club. At any rate, hopes were flying high
and we gave the Grand Master a sendoff to
remember.

I held Connie's suitcase while he fished his
ticket from his pocket. Magas, eating a hot dog,
stood by the tinted glass wall to watch the jets
taxi down the runway. Connie glanced at his
reflection in a chrome ashtray and smoothed his
thin gray-brown hair, the brown being Grecian
Formula. "Think my red shirt would have been
dressier?"

"The yellow's a better match."

Connie bought nothing but the best from
the Saint Vincent de Paul outlet. This suit was a
green-and-white-checked Edwardian number
with bedspread lapels. Judging from the weight
of this suitcase, he must have packed every other

165

stitch he owned. He started pacing in front of a row of chairs.

"Look." Magas pointed to a 747 rolling past.

All at once my hands sweated. "You got the Saint Christopher medal I loaned you?" I asked.

Connie slapped his pockets. "Left it on the dresser." He shrugged and went on pacing.

"Those birds are safe as a living room," Magas said.

I patted Connie's arm and he stood still. "Pretend you're going on the Trailways," I said.

He waved his fist and yelled, "You think I'm scared of a plane?" I stepped back and he lowered his voice. "The future of the world's on me and I'm scared sick seven grand may not get us top-notch and that maybe I should go for ten, fifteen."

It seemed business was all the Grand Master worried about. It could it be that Mr. Skupas cared more about the mission than even himself, which was a way of saying about me too. Come to think of it, he hadn't even firmed up if he was taking me to the VFW mixer. Crusade, crusade, was all he thought. A Knight is one thing, a fanatic's another.

"Quarter of a million?" he asked.

I slammed down the suitcase.

"My foot!"

I moved the valise. "If seven turns out not enough you can always go back to Rome," I said.

Connie sat in an orange bucket chair and swiveled half a turn in each direction. "Go back to Rome," he said, and smiled.

An hour later we headed toward the boarding gate. Safe as living rooms, I kept telling myself. The suitcase slowed me down and Connie stopped to wait. "Not too much water at one time on my African violets," he said.

The guard, a black woman chewing gum, leaned against the wall while I swung the valise onto the conveyor belt leading into a box, a sort of x-ray machine. I asked if we could go to the gate with Connie, and the guard blew a pink bubble. It popped and she said, "Go pass security." Just as Magas stepped toward the detector-arch she pointed to his chest. The sequins flashed. "Them metal?"

"We'll stay here," Magas said quickly.

I wanted to say all the important things at once. "Don't eat anything not boiled," I said.

This was goodbye. Connie kissed Magas on both cheeks. The wizard turned and pretended to wipe a spot off his shoe. Connie sounded as if he had a cold. "I love you," he said to me. He glanced at the guard, kissed my cheek, then shot down the ramp. If Magas heard he didn't let on.

His second night in Rome, Connie called to tell me his stars were clicking. The Via Condotti was full of wine, accordion music—. I interrupted to ask how his stomach was holding. Just before the connection went bad he said the

167

Pepto-Bismol had done the trick.

The rest of the week my nerves were shot. It was all I could do to water Connie's plants every day and run his shirts through the heavy-duty cycle. The afternoon he was supposed to land in New York, I sat glued to the phone. Magas had stopped by to see if I needed company on the drive. An hour passed, then two, still no word. I checked and the Alitalia flight had been on time. So was the connecting flight to Baltimore. Could I have gotten the days mixed up? We agreed Magas would stay by my telephone and I would go to Connie's to maybe find a copy of the itinerary.

Connie's efficiency is on the third floor of the old Merchant Seamen's Hotel. The street lamp shines on his window beside the letter "M" painted on the bricks. I pulled out my key and went into his room. Mr. Skupas might as well live in a greenhouse. Ivy dangles from pots bracketed to the woodwork and climbs the iron bedposts. Alongside his footlocker, snake plants poke up among the begonias like bayonets. The only light came from a "Gro-Bulb" over a row of cactus shoots, the streetlamp, and rays of yellow, then blue neon flashing from Kobrick's Supper Club across the street.

It took me a minute to realize Connie was slumped in his rocker beside the window. I reached for the wall switch and Connie said, "Don't." I walked over and stood beside him. A yellow beam lit his rumpled jacket and a grain of rice on his tie. His solidarity button was upside down. "I took a taxi," he said.

I moved a Sunday paper and sat on the edge of the bed. "What did the Pope say?"

A wet breeze blew through the screen bringing in the smell of cloves from the McCormick Spice Company. Connie played with the ring on the window blind cord. "I didn't get the money."

"Why?"

His hand winding the cord over the ring was green in the blue light. "Too many people around to ask."

"What people?"

"One. Maybe two thousand."

I couldn't face him remembering the excitement, the high hopes at the sendoff. "How will you explain?"

The cord snapped and I looked up. Connie flipped the ring in the palm of his hand. "A setback, that's all." He leaned to pitch the ring in the wastebasket. "Now that I know how the Vatican works, next time I'll have an official appointment." His voice got stronger. "And like Petronas said, we can raise the money. In a month I'll go back, that's all."

"You got to repay Zapp."

Connie stopped rocking. Then he started up again and said, "Everything will be all right on that score, too."

"But if you never talked to the Pope—"

"It's taken care of."

I stepped back and gave him a narrow stare. He must have seen it because he struggled to his feet and headed across the room. I followed him to his opened suitcase on top of the dresser. "What are you looking for?"

He rummaged through the shadowy pile of underwear, magazines, and tiny bars of hotel soap, then handed me a cardboard square. A vial was stapled to the center. I barely made out a picture of the Pope. The writing over his head was in Italian, Latin for all I knew. "Holy water," Connie said.

I tipped the vial to see how much was in it. "So what?" I said, "You can buy one of these in the Blessed Name bookstore on Charles Street."

"Not personally from Rome."

The blue light blackened the lines along his nose making his face look sharp and mean. "Zapp will get his money's worth," he said.

I wasn't sure what Connie was driving at. "How? He should bless his business do-it-yourself?"

Connie leaned over my shoulder and tapped the edge of the cardboard. He was breathing hard. "Don't even have to be Zapp. It could be anybody. The water's what does it."

I couldn't believe what he was saying. "A proxy job?"

"I was there," Connie shouted.

"That make you the Pope?"

We stared at each other until Connie looked

at the floor. Then he turned, took the vial and dropped it back on the pile of socks. His cheeks seemed withered and soft in the yellowy glow. "You don't understand," he said quietly.

"I understand ripoff."

Connie lifted his head. He squared his shoulders and shook his finger at me. "You don't understand beans," His eyes burned. "I'm a holy messenger, a soldier in the service of the Church of Rome."

"Since?"

"Don't laugh." He held his arms straight out and cupped his hands. "I'm holding the destiny of my whole world."

I walked around him towards the door. "Magas is waiting for me," I said. Quick as a silverfish, Connie slipped in front of me, shoved a box in my palm and wrapped my fingers around it. I tried to give it back but he blocked my hand. I said goodbye and stepped into the musty hall, then hurried down the stairs past the night clerk, and didn't look back until I hit Conkling Street.

From the top of the hill I could see the shiny Baltimore harbor; the words "Domino Sugar" from the plant on the opposite shore reflected upside down. My street dead-ends at the park where despite the drizzle, Tommy Pielzck was bouncing his ball under the streetlight and shooting baskets through the ring—the net part having been gone for years. Even at night my place is cheerful what with the lace curtains and the statue of Our Lady of Sil-uva in the window. My front door was open. The theme song from MASH drifted from the living room. Magas was sitting in my Bar-calounger where I left him except he had helped himself to a can of Carling's and was spearing the last pickled herring from the jar with a toothpick. Instead of his Sūduva vest he wore a varsity sweater over his T-shirt. I turned down the sound on the TV. "Connie didn't get the money."

Magas held the toothpick midair. "Did the Pope give a reason?"

I took off my damp net scarf and spread it on the radiator. My back still turned, I said, "Vatican politics."

To this minute I don't know why I put it that way. Maybe I was protecting Connie. Once I got to talking, Magas would have wormed out the holy water story and I figured Connie would want to keep that business hush-hush. But wasn't I throwing Connie to the dogs anyway by leaking his failure before he could soft-soap the Knights into thinking it wasn't so bad? I sat across from Magus on the velveteen sofa. He pushed the lever and the back of the lounger rose. "Your eyes look funny," he said.

"Hay fever." I reached in my purse for a tissue.

He lowered his head. Hands between his knees, he dented the empty can with his thumbs. "Losing is worse on the auxiliary," he said.

I nodded and blew my nose at the same time."

"To work like a dog and still have no say," Magas said. He raised his chin. "But Connie can go back and try another time."

All at once I decided to mention something I'd been meaning to mention for a long time. "Sometimes I think Connie's kidding himself, and us too." Then I added, "Do you agree with him?"

Magas gripped the arms of the chair to help himself up. "Sure," he said, then added the clinker, "Same as you."

I wondered if Magas meant yes, he agreed. Or sometimes yes, sometimes no, same as me? Or if he saw more agreement in me than I knew about myself. I decided not to push the issue as I walked him to the door. He held onto the banister with one hand, and his stick with the other, and inched down my concrete steps. "Ciao," he said.

I slowly closed the front screen. Then I felt a lump in my sweater pocket and pulled out Connie's present. The box wasn't wrapped and I took off the lid. A cameo pin, the size of a quarter, with a gray face against a black sky stared up at me. The lady smiled, but the looking part of her eye was just a little hole. Funny, it seemed the longer I held her the heavier she got.

The next meeting of the Knights was two

weeks away. Not that I was laying low from Mr. Skupas, but my number four dryer was blowing cold only, and I had to monkey with the heating unit. Meanwhile, I figured the news that Connie came back empty-handed would be getting around. Every morning Magas buys coffee and a chocolate doughnut from Zebnick's Bakery where Joe's kid, Anna, works. Anna rents Vito's second floor. Vito and Petronas carpool to High-landtown Motors where Louie's a sheet-metal man.

The day of the Knights meeting, I left dryer parts spread out on newspaper so to get to Novotsky's on time. I finished setting up the long folding table just as Geminaikas, the last to come in, took his seat. Tension hung in the air like grease smoke. One minute after seven the Grand Master shoved the curtain aside and everyone stood. Connie did not look my way, but from the corner of my eye I saw he was wound up like a spring. During the Puntukas reading, he kept craning his neck to see around Magas who blocked the view to the doorway. The poem over, Connie shifted from one foot to another and looked at his watch. Just then the curtain shimmied, hung still, then slid open, you could have blown me over like a feather. Dominic Zappardino stood in the entrance, hat in hand.

Connie whipped out a chair and patted the seat. Zappardino made his way across the room and sat down. His round face was scrubbed pink. He wore a tan jacket with an alligator over his heart and carried a golf cap. The crease in his jeans had been ironed in. He had this habit— nerves I guess—of laughing, then stopping the laugh midstream.

"As you know," Connie began, "I just got back from Rome where I had an interesting and informative visit." He sounded like the Pope's letter. "By now you are aware that, due to cir- cumstances, the Pope was not able to see his way clear at this time to provide our fiduciary. How- ever," Connie went on, "enough old news, now for the new news. Zapp?"

Zapp stood, and crossed his arms across his chest, his cap showing under one elbow. "Mr. Skupas asked me to drop by in person to speak to your organization." Then Zapp made a joke about the weather while me—and I bet every other Knight in the room—was crazy to know what Connie was up to.

"Beyond my wildest dreams," Zapp was saying. "I ask for a simple blessing, to make everything kosher. It turns out the minute the Pope touches my papers, allowing, of course, for time change back on this side of the pond, all hell breaks loose." Zapp's eyes narrowed and his voice turned all business. "The city zones my Patapsco River frontage high density. Then the County comes along and says they're cutting an I-95 spur alongside my forty acres at the mall. And the same day I, that is, De Vencenzio's Construction and me, got a development loan to break ground on the entertainment arcade."

Mafalda Zappardino was a De Vencenzio. It dawned on me that Zapp, his old man a vegetable huckster swinging up and down cobbly Homestead Avenue, would be a millionaire. "All this thanks to Mr. Skupas using his influence on my behalf," Zapp said.

Connie ducked his head and shrugged.

"Whatever you guys are doing I just know one thing," Zapp fumbled in the pocket of his checkered shirt. "You don't get nothing unless you pay back first." He held up a check. "Zappardino Incorporated would like to donate to the Knights of Pontucko, the ten thousand dollars for your special project."

Connie, grinning ear to ear, bowed as he took the check. He and Zapp shook hands. Zapp started to sit, then stood. "Deductible," he mumbled as if suddenly embarrassed. He laughed and sat down quick.

You could have heard a pin drop. Then the Knights clapped, cheered, and pounded each other on the back. More thoughts than I could think at the same time raced through my head. Zapp had been swindled. Not that he looked it, holding up the Stolichnaya bottle and saying, "Great stuff." On the other hand, to me Connie's face looked darker and more pinched. What good are Knights who mess with the standards of the brotherhood? Zapp, any man has the right to know exactly where his blessing stood. Maybe I should level with him before the check was cashed.

Connie slapped me on the shoulder. "What do you say, Maruta?"

"You better thank Mr. Zappardino."

At that point the meeting disintegrated. Irena brought in the kugelis and Magas invited her to hang around. Novotsky himself stuck his head in the door to see why the noise, then washed down the last of the potatoes with a few shots and a beer. I overheard Connie say to Zapp, "For our consultant, only the best think-tank in Washington."

Around midnight Novotsky started closing down. The Knights decided to finish the party at the Sportsmen's Club next door. I said I'd be along in a minute. Connie, like always, hung back to polish off the vodka while I circled the table using crumpled napkins to wipe up spills. He poured out what was left in the bottle, shook it, then held it to the light. My green plastic bag was almost full, but I stuffed in a few more paper plates and reached for a twister. "It crossed my mind," I said, "to mention to Zapp about the proxy."

Connie stared at me, his pale eyes more watery than usual. "The blessing took, didn't it?" He ran his finger around the rim of his glass. "You know what else?" I emptied an ash-tray on the paper tablecloth and rolled it up. Connie's voice was soft. "I been thinking about the night I came back and how you don't under-stand nothing." He finished the vodka in one swallow, then wiped his mouth. "I figured out what it all boils down to between you and me."

I nodded at the empty bottle. "Please, in the bag."

"You're not listening."

"What it all boils down to between you and me."

He dropped the bottle on top of Irena's tinfoil tray in the green sack. "It all boils down to whether you agree with me or not."

Trapped like a rat, I didn't have the stomach to lie. But since I myself didn't know the truth I couldn't level. I wrapped the twister around the neck of the bag. "Who could agree with your sneaky ways?"

He thought for a minute, then slapped his palm on the table. "Zappardino."

I walked beside Connie to the vestibule between the curtain and the back door. "My ways have to suit my ways, that's all," He said. "Speaking of which, we on or off for the VFW?"

A month ago I would have been on cloud nine inside. But this new Mister Skupas goes around doing proxys. On the other hand, maybe Connie did right. People say everything has its own special reason, like when a poor man kills a chicken one of them is sick, or you can't make blynai without breaking eggs. "What VFW?"

"I have mixer tickets."

"Paid for?"

"Since a long time."

"In that case."

He gave me a peck on the cheek, then stood

with his hand on the knob. "You be by the Sportsmen's?" I nodded and he closed the door behind him.

I looked around the back room, checking my cleanup job. Not through. The banner still hung on the wall. Standing on a chair I started to pull out the thumbtacks, then changed my mind and climbed down. Our banner is like the one carried by the Knights of Kaunas in the old days. In the center is the Vytas, the Knight symbolizing the Grand Duchy of Lithuania. Above him, Snake Osier is twisted to spell Musti, but it's perfectly clear he's gliding straight to the Holy City. I told Connine it seemed funny that a little gray snake should be taking off to Jerusalem. But Connie says snakes are messengers from heaven. They shed their skin to honor the Resurrection. That's why Osier wears a crown. And if that's the case, who am I to argue?

TEN

Gurlas

Every day after school, Elena fired up the furnace. If the coals died and the water pipes froze and burst, she would be to blame. Each time she stepped into the cellar she remembered Papa's threats. The dripping cement-block walls that smelled like mushrooms seemed to lean closer. When she pulled the string dangling from the ceiling light, roaches—quick brown needles—darted down the drain in the floor. She felt them watching her with their mica eyes, hating her for intruding, waiting for their chance to get even.

The furnace sat like an emperor in the center of the room. In raised letters across its iron door, the word "Matterlink" shone. Elena would unlatch the gate to the coal bin, a dark, wide coffin. She was barely able to see the heap of anthracite skulls. She would toss a shovelful of coal into the fiery mouth, slam the door, then

181

glance to the far corner of the basement. A curtain hid Uncle Lezek's bed. Holding her breath she listened for a rustle, the squeak of springs. She wondered where Uncle Lezek's strange friend, Gurlas, was. Uncle Lezek told her Gurlas lived with him. She wondered if he lied.

Last year, when she was eight, Uncle Lezek had hitchhiked to West Virginia. Laid off from a mine in Pennsylvania, he had come to Shackle looking for work. The first night he ate supper with Elena and Papa he drew a watch from his hip pocket, checked the time, then snapped the case shut. Elena stared. He dangled the timepiece from its golden chain over his plate of cabbage. It hung like a full amber moon.

"Do you polish that watch every day?" she asked.

Uncle Lezek stiffened, as if shocked. "Someone does that for me."

Holding his fork like a trowel, Papa ate without looking up.

"A slave?" she asked.

Lezek tucked the watch in his pocket and laughed. "A friend," he said.

She pushed a caraway seed to the side of her bowl. "What's your friend's name?"

Lezek lowered his glass of whiskey, then glanced at the ceiling and snapped his fingers. "Gurlas."

"Where is Gurlas?" she asked.

Lezek shrugged. "Who can say?" He nodded at the screendoor. "Maybe outside."

She craned her neck to look at the back porch.

"Eat," Papa ordered.

"I don't see anyone," she complained.

Lezek leaned towards her and asked in a low voice, "Can you see the bit in the mouth of lightning?" He pointed to the window. "The words of branches talking to their trees?"

Her eyes widened.

Papa shoved his empty dish aside. "Hey Lezek, you find work yet?"

Lezek winked at Elena and said, "Magic."

A week later, Papa, a long-wall operator at PAW, Pittsburgh and Wierton Industries, got Lezek a job as a rock duster. Paper told Lezek he could room at their house.

Lezek brought only his supply of long thin cigars and the steamer trunk that he and Papa had dragged from Vilnius twenty years ago. Elena wondered where Lezek would sleep. The kitchen and bedrooms of their four-room company house overflowed with the supplies Papa used to make whiskey. Burlap sacks of barley leaned against every wall.

Papa liked to tell the story about the day he was poking around an auto graveyard for a Chevy transmission and spotted a battered copper still hidden in the weeds behind a tractor. The notion of selling whiskey, he said, tore through his brain like a golden bullet. He untangled the honeysuckle vines from the copper coils and tossed the still, mash tub and all, into the bed of his pickup truck. At home, he installed the cooker beside the kitchen stove. When he decided to refill his stock, he'd send Elena to the PAW store with a note for three twenty-pound bags of sugar. Should anyone look at her funny, she was to say her Papa was making jelly. If word leaked out and the federal agents came to the house, it would be her fault, he warned. She suspected everyone in Shackle knew what he was up to. Nonetheless, he would be sure the sheet was tacked tightly over the window before he fired up the mash.

Suppose the Giglianos next door called the police, Elena wondered. Surely she couldn't be to blame for something Mr. Gigliano did. Or could she? Perhaps all the wrongness in the world was her fault. She stared into the oatmeal-thick mash which rumbled and popped. Steam billowed from the tub, loosened the corners of the checkered wallpaper, fogged the mirror over the kitchen sink where Pops shaved. Whiffs of boiling grain that smelled like butterscotch drifted as far as the parlor. She once asked, "What if Mr. Gigliano smells whiskey coming from under our door?"

Papa was ladling the mash into oak barrels to ferment. His hand, holding a cup, paused midair. Slowly, he turned and stared down at her. His eyes were gray and slanted over high cheekbones. The skin on his jowls was sallow and crinkled as asbestos siding. She knew he dyed his hair. Under the sink, she had found a toothbrush with matted black bristles next to a bottle of Roux.

He dipped the cup back into the barrel. His voice was harsh. "Gigliano will only smell smells that you mention."

Filled with fermenting brew, the barrels were stored in the bedrooms. Elena would sit on the edge of her bed and imagine the greedy yeast feeding off the grain. She pictured the yeast granules as tiny yellow pigs with dragon snouts. She flopped back on the bed and closed her eyes. She could almost hear lips smack as the pigs stuffed themselves with plate after plate of bubbling gruel. Their stomachs bloated, showing milky skin between bristles. The skin tightened, stretched, swelled—then exploded into a galaxy of shredded barley pearls. She would open her eyes and gaze around the room, reassured by the click of the maple branch upon the window, the silent barrels lined against the wall.

The day Uncle Lezek came to stay, Papa showed off the kitchen, bedrooms, the bathroom, the toilet with no seat. He saved the parlor for last. It was used for company or when Father Vytautas came to bless the house. Three platform rockers circled an oval braided rug. A table, its marble top supported by a walnut lyre, sat under the window. The maple chair in the corner was straight-backed with a matchbook wedged under one leg. Papa had turned to Lezek and motioned to the room. "Is just for show."

"You sure you got space for me?" Lezek asked.

Papa stretched out his arm, as if offering Lezek the Baltic Sea. "The basement," he said. "No one to bother you."

Uncle Lezek stood in the kitchen. "I'm too much trouble." He ran his finger around the sheepskin collar of his denim jacket. He smiled, his square teeth blackened in spots, like dice. His eyes, slanted as Papa's, were gray shale. But Lezek's rosy cheeks were round. "Too much trouble, right Elena?" He accented the first "E" of her name.

Papa pulled out a chrome chair and patted. "What's this trouble? You're my brother, that's all."

Lezek reached into his pocket for a wad of bills. He licked his thumb and counted out the first month's room and board.

Papa picked at the snap on his shirt sleeve. "Not right to take money from family."

Lezek thrust out the bills. "What's the big difference? I pay for Mrs. Kovelesky's boarding house? I pay you." He winked at Elena. "Buy the kid piece of candy. New dress."

Elena glanced at Papa and blushed. Maybe the tear under the arm of her school uniform showed. She wished she could sew. She stepped into the shadow of the refrigerator.

Without counting them, Papa tucked the bills into his breast pocket. "Anyway, it's good you're here. Since my Maruta died, place is a cave."

Except that Maruta, Elena's mother, was not dead. Elena remembered the sounds—breaking glass and shouts—of five years ago as if they had happened yesterday. Elena had lain awake and stared past the barrels at the snail's track of silver light under her door. Papa's voice was loud, then soft as the echo of a barking dog. That year Mother's Day came and went. Papa did not take Elena to the five and ten. They used to pick out a pot of tulips that Ma set on the marble table for the neighbors to see. Ma took to her bed. Each morning Elena got herself up for school. She taught herself how to braid her long brown plait. Papa would slice salami for her breakfast and keep her company while she washed it down with Coke.

One day the bedroom door was open. Ma was gone. Elena, stricken, asked where she was.

"She took sick and died," Papa mumbled.

"What kind of sick? When?" There were a thousand questions. "Why didn't—"

Papa loomed over her. His shadow blackened her clear blue eyes. "You strangled her to death. You, you the rag in her throat."

"I never—" she sobbed.

He stepped towards her and lifted his hand. She cringed, already feeling the slap. He dropped his arm.

A few days later, Elena overheard Mrs. Gigliano shout to the mailman, "Maruta Silvuronis? Send her mail to the Starlight Motel."

Uncle Lezek fixed up his corner of the cellar. First, he strung a clothesline between the outside wall and the coal bin. Then, he hung fiberglass curtains that glistened from the line. Papa had forbidden her to go near the room. But once, home alone, she peeked behind the draperies. The cot was made up with a white chenille spread. His suit hung in a metal cabinet. Elena turned to the steamer trunk. A padlock dangled from the clasp. Gurlas must be in there.

The next day she asked Lezek more questions about Gurlas. Immaculate Conception School was only a block away and she was home for lunch. When Papa was at the mine, she and Lezek (who worked the night shift) rummaged through the refrigerator and ate whatever they found.

"Could Gurlas live in a place without air?" she asked.

Lezek held the slender cigar between his teeth and squinted at her through the smoke. "Gurlas don't breathe."

"Sister Marie says everybody has the spirit of breath," Elena said primly.

"Gurlas is not everybody."

Lezek stood at the kitchen table. His bald head was a beige mushroom. His hair had thinned to a dark brown ruffle behind each ear. A tall, burly man, he wore a T-shirt, Levis, and cowboy boots. He made a circle around his bony nose with his thumb and fingers. "Has a ruby here instead."

He bent over the copper and green smoked

herring on the table. Its gummy eye focused on the ceiling. He lifted the gill, then gently stroked the scales and whispered, "Shines like cupola."

"I'm hungry," Elena said.

Lezek jerked up his head and reached for a knife.

"I would like the part a little bit above the tail, please."

Lezek whacked off the tail and slid it towards her on butcher paper. Coal dust lined the knuckles of his pale hands. His fingers were turnips, freshly dug.

"Does Gurlas eat herring?" she asked.

Lezek frowned. "I must ask her."

Elena slapped down her fork. "Yesterday you called her a him," she said indignantly.

"Him. Her. Is no difference." He flicked an ash on top of the fish bones.

She folded her paper napkin. "That doesn't make any sense."

Lezek waved his fork in an arc over his head. "Gurlas makes Gurlas sense."

"But everyone has to be either a man or a lady."

He leaned and poked her forehead with his finger. "Only inside your idea." He stretched his arms wide, and wiggled his fingers as if feeling for words. "The idea of Gurlas is big as the North Pole. The Holy Ghost."

I wish Papa would let me go in your room." She sighed. "You could introduce me to Gurlas."

Lezek slid the horseradish across the table and smiled. "Someday. Who knows? Could be our business only." He leaned over her and tapped his chest. "Yours and mine."

The next day after school, Elena fired up Matterlink. She propped the shovel against the coal bin wall, brushed a smudge off her jumper, then checked a scab on her knee.

Lezek's voice sailed from behind the curtain. "That you Elena?" Not waiting for an answer, he said, "Kick up the damper."

She pulled the chain.

"You still out there?" he asked.

"Yes sir."

"Give me hand."

She took a step towards his corner, then paused.

"You coming or aren't you?"

"Papa said—"

Lezek's voice was impatient. "He would make you come if I needed help."

Lezek lay on the cot, the bedspread tucked around his waist. Elena stared at his chest. Gray hairs hung like a mop turned upside down over his nipples.

He lowered the Screenview magazine. Brooke Shields swam across the cover. "Help me look at movie stars," he said, patting the mattress. He propped up the magazine again. "Says here—" Lezek frowned and pointed to the words under the photo. "I don't read American so good."

She bent to see where his finger pointed.

"Sit, before you fall over," he said.

She perched on the edge and spoke the words under each caption. After a few pages, the movie stars bored her. "Where's Gurlas?"

"Sleeping," Lezek said. He reached down and adjusted the bedspread. "But maybe waking up soon."

She pointed to the trunk. "Could you let Gurlas out now?"

Lezek chuckled. "No Gurlas in there."

The back of her neck felt cold. "I have to check the fire."

Lezek held her arm. His voice was harsh. "Just a minute." In one swift maneuver, he gripped the back of her jumper and pulled her down. Her left arm was pinned beneath her. Lifting his leg, he shoved away the bedclothes.

She screamed.

His naked thighs were parted. She caught a glimpse of lavender flesh, swollen taut, before he clamped her right hand around it. His skin was hot and smooth against her palm. "Let me go," she yelled.

He squeezed his hand over hers. Eyes closed, he moved her fist in rhythm with his hips. She lunged, ready to sink her teeth into his arm. He held her off.

"I'm telling Papa," she yelled.

Gasping, he arched his back. With all her strength, she pulled her left arm free and swung at his face. He ducked, letting go of her. She

191

squirmed from his reach. "Mrs. Gigliano will go get Papa right now," she panted.

Lezek leaped, grabbed her wrists, and twisted her arms behind her. She landed face down on the bed. "You're hurting me," she cried.

He eased his grip. She lay still. Warm against her neck, his breath smelled of cigars. He spoke in her ear. "Go tell Papa. And you know what he'll say? Anybody would have accident if dirty little girl bothers them, comes right into their room."

Her heartbeat slowed. Tears burned her throat. She rubbed her nose on the flannel sheet that smelled like Vitalis.

"Elenuta," Lezek whispered.

"I didn't do anything."

"You will be punished," he said.

Her shoulders slumped. He set her free and sat on the edge of the bed. She struggled to rise, but her spine was stiff. She lay staring at the floor. A quick movement along the coal bin wall caught her eye. She raised her chin. Lezek's head was bowed. When he caught her glance, he yanked the bedspread over his lap. Coughing, he reached for his cigars on top of the trunk.

She swung her feet over the edge of the cot. Without looking at her sticky palm, she wiped it on the sheet.

Something silver shot beneath her sneaker. "What's that?"

Lezek's gaze followed her finger. "Just a little roach."

Her arms wrapped around her waist, she leaned forward. "It's white."

He laughed. "Sure. They breed in coal bin. No sunshine, fresh air."

Saliva welled in her mouth. She waited until her stomach calmed before swallowing.

"Not many of these little beauties," he added.

She opened her eyes and spotted another pale insect near the leg of the cot. Tucking the spread around him, Lezek crouched on the floor. With the cigar box, he blocked the roach's path. "See how smart? That little bugger runs straight around."

Elena trembled.

Lezek twisted his head and looked up at her. "Don't be scared. Is Gurlas, that's all."

She gripped the iron headboard and stood.

Lezek rose, the spread trailing like a wedding dress. "They live like czars." Eagerly, he pointed to one crawling under the curtain. "Only the best. Riding amber horses, sailing ships." She backed away from the bed.

"Skating too," he said, his voice desperate. "On rolling shoes made of pearls."

She pulled the curtain aside. Staring at the floor, she wiped her cheek with the back of her hand. "Liar," she whispered. The roach near her toe waved its antennae.

"What?" Lezek asked.

She looked up. His gray eyes looked injured. Drawing her braid over her shoulder she said, "Liar." She lifted her foot.

"Wait," Lezek yelled.

Just as the bug started towards the wall, she brought her heel down. The corrugated shell cracked beneath her weight.

She spun and ran from the room. Ahead, the furnace loomed like a grandfather. She grabbed the return-air duct. A minute later, she stopped shaking. She ran her fingers over the word "Matterlink," then pressed her forehead against its warm iron stomach. "Liar, liar."

"It's true." Lezek called from behind the curtain. "Gurlas has eyes of diamond chips. Forever watching you."

⟨⟨ ELEVEN ⟩⟩

Fifty Years of Eternal Vigilance

Aldonna glanced up at the jagged glass cemented into the cemetery wall and wondered who would want to be dead in a place like this. A sign, "Property of Shackle, West Virginia," swung from the iron gate. Beyond the bars, tombstone molars decayed in crooked rows along the muddy walk. She winced at a rectangle of freshly dug clay. On top, a styrofoam urn rested on its side. Plastic lilies, spattered with cinders, lay around a tin can. Shaking her head, she turned and hurried to the end of the block. While she waited for the light to change, she reminded herself that this was the kind of grave she would have. She should have gotten married, had kids to put flowers around her tomb.

As she neared the sagging porch of Charlie Spivak's funeral home, she thought she saw Charlie at the window. Sure enough, the lace curtain dropped; then he was at the screen door. The evening sun fired his garnet tiepin into an ambulance light. "Miss Kumas," he called from the top of the rickety steps. "Can you please change my regular order to pumpernickel?"

"First thing tomorrow."

"Hot enough for you?" he asked.

Thinking he might have a minute, she strolled up to the stoop. "Mister Spivak?"

He stepped down one step.

"Any one of us," she snapped her fingers, "could go like that."

He stared over her shoulder at Perpetual Savings and Loan. "You're no spring chicken."

"Do me favor."

He frowned.

She pointed back to the cemetery. "How can a person hold their head up buried in there?"

"True," he sighed.

"I want flowers every week, piney branches at Christmas, ribbons."

"Ribbons?"

Her eyes sparkled. "Pink ones tied from my headstone to the ginko tree, blue and gold strung to the railing."

Charlie leaned towards her and the ambulance light went out. "I order your coffin with holy pictures on it. Find pallbearers to walk with their arms crossed behind each other's back like in old country. Even talk Father Xawery into leading with a banner of Our Lady." He drew back. "My job is funerals. Graves outside my jurisdiction."

"Such a small favor."

He looked at his watch. "A man is only so big."

"Good night, Mr. Spivak," she said stiffly, turning onto the sidewalk.

What is this jurisdiction, she fumed, trudging over the crumbling pavement to her front door. Complete death is his business like bread is mine. People want caraway seeds? I toss them in. Glossy crust? Who counts every egg?

She unlocked her front door. The living room smelled like a root cellar. But in August all Shackle houses, barges, even fire hydrants were campgrounds for the armies of spores that marched from the dregs of the Monongahela River. She tossed her net scarf on the radiator, snapped on the kitchen overhead light, and opened the refrigerator. She skimmed off the tallow crust over last night's cabbage soup and stirred the long gray leaves.

The next morning, sunbeams discovered new decay that had crept through the night. A water bug scurried over a felt cap of moldy hair that covered the shower drain. Another varicose vein flowing under the skin of Aldonna's calf had broken into swollen tributaries. Elastic stockings don't do no good, she thought, swinging her legs over the side of the bed. Streamliner corsets no good either, she grumbled, as she fished in the chiffonier for a foundation garment. She had bought the complete line from a door-to-door saleslady—confidential. But it was no secret her figure was too important for the navy dress she squeezed into. She clamped her glasses to the chain around her neck and headed downstairs for coffee. A few minutes after the cup was rinsed, her heels clicked past Spivak's, beginning to stir after another grisly night among the caskets.

As she crossed the street in front of the cemetery, she noticed the path was blocked by a motorcycle. "Radas Meincoweicz and Son, Living Landscapes" was painted on the sidecar. A man with egg-white hair crouched over a crape myrtle. She hesitated. "You work for the city?"

"Tend grass for families." The r's rolled on his tongue.

She took a step forward, then turned back. "You Polish?"

"Krakov."

An idea flared like a prayer candle touched by a taper. She stooped beside him. "I'm Aldy Kumas from Kaliska. Got a minute?"

They stood up at the same time and she took a deep breath. "Twenty years ago I come here to make money, go home and open restaranja on Nowy Swiat Street." She pushed a broken brick off the path with the toe of her Red Cross oxford. "But you know what it's like there now."

Radas shrugged at the brick. "My boy never got to hear the trumpeter."

A wad of homesickness to hear the trumpet again, played on the hour over Krakov Square, clogged her throat. "I'm at the age when I'll have to die." Her eyes swept the crumbling tombs choked in weeds, "And look like those."

He cleared this throat. "Not meaning to be serious, but you could buy my service."

"Please explain."

"We got Lux-Alive and Econ-o-Trim—" A beer truck rattled past.

She pointed down the street. "You know the bakery on Wiley Avenue?" she yelled above the clatter.

"Kumas's," he shouted.

"I close up at six, but come around the alley and bang on the white door."

He snapped his pruners. "Seven sharp."

That evening at seven Aldy slid aside the yellow tablet she'd been sketching on and got up to answer the door. Radas, canvas cap in hand, beamed at her through the screen. His cheeks gleamed melon, and whiffs of vanilla shaving lotion mingled with cinnamon steam from the last batch of rolls. She tucked a loose hair under her net.

He lifted a vinyl briefcase. "Where can I set this?"

She motioned to the marble-top work table

and watched him pull out a chair. "Coffee?" she asked.

"Such bother—"

"Done already," she said, pulling the plug from the pot. The fluorescent light shone on his curly white hair, tweeded with brass, and suddenly she pushed the pot back and whipped a bottle of vodka from under the sink. Grabbing two shot glasses stored behind the mixers, she tucked the bottle under her arm and stood beside him.

He grinned up at her as she poured. "That's a man's drink," he said.

They clinked glasses. "Nazdrowie!" he shouted.

"Kills the nerve," she gasped, wiping her mouth on her wrist.

She poured him a second and sat across from him to study the mimeographed brochures that explained the maintenance service. After a few minutes, she looked up, disappointed. "I want more than routine."

"We just added statue-care. Fourteen dollars a month extra."

She slid the brochure towards him and stood.

"How much more you want?" he asked.

Knuckles on the table, she loomed over him. "Candles on All Souls, piney branches at Christmas, Easter florals."

"Reusable?"

"And ribbons," she added.

"How ribbons?"

She shoved the yellow pad in front of him and pointed to the sketch. He studied it for a minute, then frowned. "I don't do ribbons."

The room became still except for the refrigerator hum. "Then you're just a janitor-man, that's all."

Radas jumped to his feet and waved at the wall of ovens. "Better than being some tough cookie," he yelled, heading towards the door.

Mr. Meincoweicz has more pride than a falcon, she thought, motioning him to calm down. He slid back into his chair.

"Trouble with your business is, you should think complete," she said.

"Let's see that picture again," he sighed.

They passed the pencil back and forth, agreed on ribbons, piney branch arrangements, potted lilies. Finally Radas slumped back. "You some artist. This grave fancier than General Pilsudski's." He frowned and started to rub his jaw.

"Just to mention it," she said, "this will be paid for out of my will."

"I work up a price." He held a pencil over a sample contract. "For one year?"

She shook her head. "For eternity, naturally."

He slapped the pencil on the table. "I don't contract for eternity."

"So long as I'm down there I'll need extra hands on top."

"You think eternity can last forever?"

She examined her fingernail. "Then how long?"

He closed his eyes and whispered numbers, then opened them. "I suppose we could make it for life of my youngest, Joey."

"Suppose you and the missus—"

"She die nine years ago."

Aldy wondered why that information cheered her up.

Radas turned the contract towards her. "See where it says dates? Joey's ten, so we go for fifty years. He shouldn't work like his old man until he drops. Should retire to Miami."

"If that's the best you can do," she sighed.

Radas stood and rolled the contract around the sketches. "My kid Sophie can write this on the machine tomorrow."

Aldy walked around the table to see him to the door. A hot breeze that smelled like oily fish blew from the river, and crickets chirped in the weeds along the porch. "Thank you for the hospitality."

"Think nothing."

He unlatched the screen, then turned. "You bowl, Miss Kumas?"

"Possibly."

He jammed on his cap and stepped onto the creaking porch boards. "Maybe we get together next Knights of Columbus, Ladies Free Monday."

The following Monday, Aldy sat next to Radas on a leatherette sofa while he balanced a paper cup of beer on the arm. "I show your grave picture to Jim Yankovitz over at Yankee Motors and he want same thing for his mom when she dies," Radas said above the crash of pins.

Aldy bit open a mustard packet. "Why can't Jim take care of her grave himself?"

"He and the missus moving to Pittsburgh. He wants palms on Easter though and I said I'd ask you to draw it for him."

She wrapped a napkin around her hot dog. "Why me?"

"I can do the dirt work. You better up here." He tapped the side of his head. "We split profit."

She brushed a crumb off her slacks. "Don't seem right to get money to do a family's holy duty," she said.

"Caterers take care of weddings, confirmations, even golden anniversaries for families."

"True," she sighed. "I'll call Jim."

On Labor Day, Aldy was telling the cook, Crazy Anna, about Radas' service while she waited for the last batch of rye to come out of the oven. Suddenly, Anna buried her face in a dishtowel.

"Don't cry," Aldy said, gently taking the towel.

Anna's cheek, marked with a purple birthmark shaped like a crown, was smeared with tears. "I always want honorable remembrances too, like in my village." She smiled and gazed above the ovens, as if seeing a dream. "My shrine with Our Lady living in a glass case. Three birch crosses, the tallest in front like the bow of a ship. Three candles lit on the Feast of Three Kings."

"Call Mister Meincoweicz," Aldy said.

"He's seen graves in Grodnorsky?"

"I'll help you draw it for him," Aldy said as the oven timer went off.

Word spread that Radas and Aldy would make graves like in the old country. There cemeteries were jammed every afternoon with loved ones filling urns and lighting candles. Horses, hitched to the family wagons, chewed thistle beside the road while they waited. As old Mister Tovak told Aldy, "Graves are to people what flags are to nations."

By Thanksgiving, Radas had to buy a machine to answer the telephone while Sophie was in school. Aldy had piles of back orders stacked on her sideboard. But it made her feel guilty to think she'd be rich as soon as her customers died. It seemed against God's will to sell what people couldn't live without.

"Look at it this way," Radas said. "If you didn't sell people bread, they'd starve."

Crazy Anna was the first to die. As Charlie,

tiepin flashing in the November sun, herded Father and Aldy from the gravesite, Radas roared to a stop and started unloading the sidecar.

The next day, Aldy slipped away from the bakery to help erect the birch crosses to look like the bow of a ship. Joey, who should have been in school, raked the frozen lumps of clay into a garden on top of the grave.

The next Saturday, a small crowd milled around to watch Radas jockey a plaster statue of Our Lady into the glass shrine. A photo in *The Sunday Dominion*, with Radas lighting a votive candle, was captioned, "Fifty Years of Eternal Vigilance."

Two weeks later, Mister Tovak's grave sported a 12-foot-high log cross surrounded by American flags.

A week before Christmas, Radas sat beside Aldy at her dining room table while they waited for Father Xawery to come and give the holiday blessing of the house.

"He's early," Aldy said, as the doorbell rang. She shoved the shot glasses towards Radas while she whisked the vodka under the table. "Coming." She tugged the lace tablecloth down an inch on the vodka side.

Father Xawery swept into the house like a rook. "You here, too, Meincoweicz?"

Aldy blushed. "Winding up graves, that's all."

Father strode to the center of the room,

held out an arm as if multitudes knelt under it, and sprinkled holy water from the censor. Radas and Aldy, heads bowed, stood as he mumbled prayers in Polish. They looked up at the same time. Father coughed and thumped his chest.

"Sit for a little refreshment," Aldy said, bustling into the kitchen.

Father pulled out a chair. "To be polite, that's all. Very busy."

Aldy came back carrying a chrome tray holding a vodka bottle, three cut glasses, and sliced babka cake.

Father stood and held his glass up to the Tiffany chandelier. "Nazdowie," he shouted, downed the vodka, set the glass on the table, then turned to Radas. "Hear you two doing great guns on the graves."

Radas beamed. "Need to hire a mason and order a crate of candles."

Aldy frowned. Maybe I should say my worries in front of Father, she thought. "You ever think we're taking jobs away from sons and daughters?"

Father frowned. "Crazy Anna didn't have kids."

Aldy motioned to the pile of contracts on the sideboard. "We got orders for whole families. Babies."

Father brushed crumbs off his fingers. "This is America, not old country where people care."

"We're putting price tags on love."

"You came here to get rich. Now you want it this way and that way at the same time," Father said.

Aldy refilled their glasses. "Maybe I'm making a mountain," she said. They drank silently.

"Almost forgot," Father said, reaching into his cassock pocket. "Had lunch with the big shots last week at the Chamber of Commerce. This guy wants you to call him." Father handed Radas a business card.

"Skimmer Z. Bixby," Radas read aloud. "President, West Virginia Coal and Transport, Subsidiary, Bixby Industries."

"Got to run." Father stood and shook hands with Aldy, then Radas.

"What does Bixby want?" Aldy asked.

"Probably a special grave. He saw the picture in the paper."

On the feast day of the Three Kings, Aldy and Radas stood in front of the elevator in the Bixby building. Radas smoothed the collar of his motorcycle jacket. "I look dressy enough?"

"Distinguished."

Bixby's office had huge windows overlooking the Monongahela. Photographs of coal barges pushed by paddle-wheel steamers covered the wall by the door. In the center of the room, a tall glass case held a varnished oar. Aldy stooped to read the plaque on the walnut frame, "Harvard, 1971." A slender man in a blazer hopped from behind the desk and pumped Radas' hand. "Mr. Meincoweicz."

Aldy shot out her hand. "Aldonna Kumas."

Bixby motioned them towards a corner sofa, and went back behind his desk.

"Nice oar you got there," Radas said.

"Sweat off the old brow," Bixby said.

"No calls," he barked into the intercom, leaned back, swiveled a few half turns, and made his hands into a cathedral. "I understand you folks own the Eternal Vigilance Company, sell services paid for out of estates."

"Have to haul a crate of candles in my side-car," Radas said.

"Just the other day at the club I said everything's dead in this town except death," Bixby chuckled.

"Have to bring on a new man," Radas said.

"Most businesses are in a slump. Damn unions suck all the profits from the mines. The trucking industry replaced our Bixby barge service to Pittsburgh and Steubenville."

Aldy glanced at her watch. "What kind of grave do you want?"

His eyes opened wide. "You," he pointed at her, then at his chest. "think that I—?" He burst out laughing. "They'll never believe it!" he gasped.

"Then you don't want the service?" she asked stiffly.

Bixby cleared his throat. "I invited you here to discuss how you can expand your little grave business into a growth industry."

"You know a good mason?" Radas asked. Aldy poked him in the ribs with her elbow.

"I have a proposition that will eliminate your problem of consumer lag."

"What's that?" Aldy asked.

Bixby's chair squeaked as he leaned forward. "No doubt you experience considerable downtime after you negotiate a contract. Why, with bad luck, years could pass before a client was prepared to, well, let's say consume your service."

Radas frowned. "Time is in God's hands."

"I can change that," Bixby continued. "I happen to have five hundred acres of prime riverview land down towards Fairmont. An ideal location for a cemetery." He gazed at the wall above the pictures. "Suppose I put up the land and improvements. You people market lots and those—" he flipped his wrist, "services. My legal-eagles can write something up."

Radas scratched his head. "What do you think, Aldy? Suppose we could take on another cemetery?"

Bixby held up his index finger. "Wrong, Mr. Meincoweicz. Not just another cemetery. As soon as the customer signs, you and Miss Karma will establish the grave so the owners can admire it, visit it, compete with their friends."

He's giving death more time, Aldy thought. She closed her eyes for a second as a prayer shot through her mind: "Saint Michael, the Archangel, thrust into hell the evil spirits who roam through the world, seeking the ruin of souls."

Radas smiled, and she stared at him in amazement, then turned to Bixby. "We don't deal in no empties," she snapped.

Bixby focused on Radas. "We'll get Merk and Bittle to do the advertising." He spelled the letters in the air with his forefinger. "L-I-V-I-N-G-D-E-A-T-H," he said. "What could sell better?"

"But Fairmont's kind of far," Radas said. A brand-new notion of her partner swelled in Aldy's mind like yeast stirred into warm sugar water.

"We'll offer weekend packages at the Bixby Lodge."

"Might be nice for kids," Radas said.

"Especially for children, because we'll have a memory Amusement Park on the grounds," Bixby said.

While Bixby described the free-ride policy, Aldy remembered being ten and kneeling in the snow beside her mother at her father's grave. He had been one of the first Polish generals killed, part of the raggedy army that held Europe against the Nazis while the Allies drank scotch in hotels. The pieces of him had been gathered by his men from the banks of the Vistula.

"Why didn't Papa run away?" Aldy never tired of asking.

"Because Christ didn't," her mother said.

Bixby stood and rubbed his palms together. "Well folks, I'd like to go on but it's getting late.

Suppose I get some numbers on paper and we'll get together again, say Friday?"

A kleenex tumbled off Aldy's lap as she struggled to her feet. So what if I insult this Bixby zwiere, she thought. Or that other person I used to trust.

"Today is the day of the Three Kings," she said.

"Who?" Bixby asked.

"Wise men who knew the difference between what can be sold and what has to be a gift. You haven't figured out the difference between life and death. You mix up everything you touch. Except me." She walked to the door and turned to Radas. "When I met you, all you knew was how to take care of dirt. Now, with this Bixby, your business is completely complete. But same thing."

A gust of wind spun the revolving door of the Bixby building behind her. She squinted into the driving sleet and set off towards the bus stop. She would mail every cent of profit back to Radas, but she couldn't buy back her pride. Your own fault, she thought, should have known Mr. Radas was flattering your idea, not you. And you, acting like sixteen-year-old. Sure enough, her reflection in Kresge's window showed just another old woman in a worn overcoat and clear plastic boots.

She paused before fording the water churning in the gutter. A pack of matches swirled down the storm sewer and suddenly she wondered if Anna's three candles were still lit. Aldy turned towards the cemetery. Her coat was soaked, and halfway up the hill she stopped to sneeze.

The smell of fresh coffee lured her into the entrance of the luncheonette across the street from the cemetery. Beside the doorway, an old man slept on a grate enveloped in steam from the building. Aldy gingerly stepped over his legs, feet in battered jogging shoes and rags wrapped around his ankles.

Her nose ran in the sudden warmth of the luncheonette, and she wiped it on a corner of her babushka as she perched on a stool. "Coffee please, and one jelly doughnut."

The waitress pushed a mug of coffee and the doughnut on a greasy plate towards Aldy, and sauntered into the back room. Aldy stared into the mirror over the grill and wondered why she had been such a fool over Radas. Suddenly, reflected in the mirror, she saw Radas at the window. His hands cupped his eyes as he looked in over the brass rings of the cafe curtains. A minute later, he was swinging his leg over the stool beside hers. She studied his face. His smile wrinkles had turned into barbed wire lines.

"Was on my way to Anna's candles and spotted you here," he said. "Just came in to tell you one thing."

"You want to buy out my share of the business," she said.

He banged his fist on the counter. "Stop

making up my mind." He rubbed at an oil-spot on his sleeve. "After you left, I told Bixby what he could do with his oar."

She turned to him, surprised. "Why?"

He cupped his hand as if it held a weight. "All along I thought you understand Radas Meincoweicz. Maybe even like that old man." His arm dropped to his side. "True, for one minute I was tempted to go along with Bixby, but you should know my heart has more sense."

Aldy touched the soggy doughnut with the tip of her fork, then pushed the plate away. She could feel his hurt and was ashamed of herself.

"You so high and mighty, you figure I do wrong before you bother to find out if I do right," he said. She tried to explain she had made a mistake, but no sound came from her dry throat. He headed towards the door, stopped, and turned back. "I guess Eternal Vigilance businesses come and go," he said sadly.

Aldy remembered the time she slipped in the bathtub: first shock, then a careful check to see which bones were broken. Now, the bones worked but she felt an empty space in her heart. The hole was raw with jagged edges, as if something had been torn out. She pulled the plate back and bit into the greasy doughnut.

By the time she stepped into the twilight, the sleet had stopped and the night was clear. But the air felt like she had inhaled an icicle. Anna's candles became, for the moment, the only reason for Aldy being alive. Bet Radas forgot, she thought, and hurried into the cemetery. She passed Mr. Tovak's flags, and finally spotted Anna's shrine. As she had suspected, the candles were out. Aldy peered into the pine branches to check the wicks.

"That's janitor's job," Radas said. She spun around and saw his figure dwarfed by the birch crosses.

"I'm sorry I said that."

"I'll go get new candles," he said, walking towards his motorcycle parked in the shadows at the bottom of the path.

Her teeth chattered as she stared at the swaying cypress trees and the round moon, crisp as an onion slice.

Radas came back with an unopened crate of votive candles in their glass cups. He tore off the cardboard lid and took out three boxes. After he dumped out Anna's burned ones and stuck in replacements, he lit them with his cigarette lighter.

An amber glow lit Our Lady's face. Aldy followed Radas' glance to the grave next to Anna's, a ground-level slab with a name cut into the stone, as if the weight of identity kept the occupant from soaring over the cemetery as proud as Anna. Radas walked over to the box on the ground, took out a candle, and tucked the holder between the tomb and a rock. The flame warmed the brown marble into oatmeal.

Inspired, Aldy grabbed a candle and stuck it at the base of the tomb on the other side of

Anna. Radas handed her a pack of matches. Might as well light the grave behind, too, she thought reaching for the box. When she looked up to find Radas, she spotted him lighting a grave across the path.

Within a few minutes, they fell into a system of dashing for fresh boxes from the crate, scooping out niches for holders, and lighting flames. The only sound above the moaning of the wind was their fevered panting and the scrape of matches. After an hour, they only saw each other as they silently grabbed boxes. Once, as a match burned down, Aldy noticed her index finger was bleeding and her hands were matching trowels caked with mud.

Finally, she reached for a new box and found the crate empty. Radas stumbled up beside her and she put her hand on his arm. She looked at the hillside and gasped.

As far as she could see, the cemetery glowed with hundreds of flickering lights that made shadows dance in the trees. The candlelight turned each tomb into a jewel, gave light to show sparkle, but not enough to light flaws. Near the top of the hill, Anna's three crosses loomed over the flames.

Aldy's knees felt weak and she slumped against Radas. He squeezed her shoulder, then gently turned her away from the hillside, and they trudged down to where he was parked. At the bottom of the path, they looked back. A few candles had burned out, but the rest twinkled like guiding stars.

Aldy turned to the luncheonette and saw the waitress staring, with pumpkin eyes, over the cafe curtain. The man on the grate was sitting up and nodding at the hillside as if it were dawn.

Radas motioned to the back of the motorcycle. Aldy eyed the narrow seat, sighed, and yanked her dress above her knees and swung her leg over the bar. The cold prickled the skin on her thigh, and she winced at the sputter of the engine. Two false starts, and they bounced onto the street. "Hang on to me!" Radas yelled.